Notes
In
A Mirror

By

Helen Macie Osterman

Notes

In

A Mirror

By

Helen Macie Osterman

Weaving Dreams Publishing
Watseka, Illinois

Weaving Dreams Publishing

ISBN 978-0-9824876-1-7

Library of Congress Control Number: 2009928477

ALL RIGHTS RESERVED

www.weavingdreamspublishing.com

Cover Design by John E. Durkin

Printed in the United States of America
10 9 7 6 5 4 3 2

Dedication:

To nurses everywhere

Acknowledgments:

Thanks to my publisher and editor, Sue Durkin, for bringing this book to life.

To the faithful members of my writers' group, The Southland Scribes, many thanks for their input along the way.

And to John Morton, always my first reader and critic, my love and gratitude.

Introduction

Before tranquilizers became available, the mentally ill were committed to large institutions where they were supervised and protected from harming themselves and others. One of these institutions was Chicago State Mental Hospital, also known as Dunning, after the name of the man who originally owned part of the land. It was located on Chicago's northwest side.

The hospital opened in the early part of the twentieth century and officially closed in the nineteen seventies. During those years the poor, the indigent, and the insane, as the mentally ill were called, occupied the cottage wards on over one hundred and fifty acres of land. A tall wrought iron fence surrounded the entire complex. It was a self-contained world with its own treatment buildings, infirmary, power plant and bakery.

The treatments provided were primitive and sometimes dangerous, but at that time, considered *state of the art.*

Student nurses from many of the Chicago and suburban nursing schools spent three months at Dunning for their psychiatric training. That was a time most of them never forgot. The author was one of those students.

Today the mentally ill are no longer committed to large institutions. New buildings dot the original grounds of the state hospital. The Chicago-Read Mental Health Center is one of a number of State Community Centers utilizing today's accepted concepts. The aim is to return patients to the community as soon as possible using medications, psychotherapy, and rehabilitation techniques.

The corner formerly occupied by Chicago State Mental Hospital now holds a shopping center erected where the entrance was located. It is called Dunning Square and is designed like every other strip mall featuring a Jewel, Osco, TJ Max, Burger King and Dunkin Donuts.

This story is fiction. Hillside Mental Hospital is based on the original Chicago State Hospital and the treatments described were those accepted at the time.

Prologue

The child gripped the pencil in her left hand. She began the first clumsy strokes at the right edge of the tablet. She wrote slowly at first, then faster as the letters formed on the paper. The words were not legible, at least not as they appeared.

But when she held the tablet up to the mirror, the message was perfectly clear.

My name is Mary Louise Hammond.
I am eight years old.

Mary Louise shook her head to clear away the fuzzy feeling. Why did this happen to her? It was happening more often. She remembered her first attempts at writing. She was naturally left-handed, but Mother said it was not lady-like for a girl to be left-handed. Mother said it was not normal. It was the devil's work. Mary Louise must learn to use her right hand just like all the other children, other- wise they would laugh at her. She must do it to please Mother.

She had tried so hard. Her first attempts were only scribbles. The teacher scolded. Mother scolded. The child cried. Eventually she learned to do what everyone wanted. She was always eager to please except when she was alone. Then she would pretend. She put the pencil in her left hand. It felt so natural that way. Then she wrote her name, backwards. When she held it up to the mirror, it was regular writing. The game was such fun. Mary Louise pretended there was another little girl, just like her, in the mirror. This child lived in a left-handed world. Everything was backwards. Mary Lou spent many hours playing this game. The house was lonely on cold winter nights with no brothers or sisters to play with, and no pets, either. Mother didn't like animals.

Worst of all there was no daddy.

"We don't talk about him," Mother said. "He was a bad man. He went away and left us alone."

Mary Louise's friend in the left-handed world had a daddy. He was left-handed, too.

One day Mother found Mary Louise playing her game. She saw her writing backwards and heard her talking to her friend in the mirror. Mother was so angry she smashed the mirror. She slapped Mary Louise's hand so hard that it turned red. The child cried until there were no more tears. She put away her left-handed world and did what her mother wanted.

Chapter 1

Chicago, Illinois, 1950

Bill Parker stopped the car at an intersection on the outskirts of Chicago. In the gloom Mary Lou Hammond had her first glimpse of Hillside State Mental Hospital. The larger buildings loomed before them, dark and foreboding. The smaller cottage type structures sprawled along one side and back into the filmy distance. Except for an occasional lighted window, they appeared uninhabited. The grounds may have been pretty in summer. Now they slumbered mysteriously under a blanket of falling snow. The place took on a feeling of unreality: a sense of past, present and future, all at once. A guard stopped them at the gatehouse, which was the only visible opening in the tall imposing wrought iron fence surrounding the acreage.

"Your ID," the man said.

"What?" Bill asked. "I didn't hear you."

"Identification," the man shouted above the howling wind. "We don't let just anybody in here. There's no visiting hours today. State your business or git."

Mary Lou's trembling fingers held out her hospital ID tag. "I'm one of the student nurses checking in for my psychiatric rotation," she said as loud as she could.

The guard looked at the tag, blew out a breath, and pointed. "The nurses' dorm is that way. I lock the gate at ten, so, if you don't leave by then, Sonny, ya'll have to stay here with the loonies." His laugh came out as a low guttural sound.

Bill nodded as he rolled up the window. "Pleasant fellow."

"Oh Bill, this place is so scary." Mary Lou clutched her boyfriend's arm. "I wish I didn't have to stay here."

"Come on, Hon, it can't be that bad. He's just an old fart. Probably gets his kicks out of scaring the students. Before you know it the three months'll be over, and I'll be picking you up to go home."

Mary Lou couldn't shake a feeling of something ominous. A heavy pall lay over the grounds. Shadows loomed everywhere. The howling wind sounded like a lost soul crying in the gloom. She shook her head to rid herself of the strange sensations.

Bill pulled up to a building looking very much like the rest: long, low, and drab. They squinted to see the sign, *Nurses Home*, over the door. A weak bulb, blinking and threatening to go out at any moment, provided the only illumination. Some light shone through the windows, but it was not a welcoming sight. It wasn't soft and warm, but harsh and cold. Mary Lou shivered, dreading the next twelve weeks.

Bill parked the car next to the entrance and took her luggage out of the trunk. "Are you getting out or have you decided to stay in the car?" he asked.

She sat, unable to move, until he opened the door and gently took her arm.

"Come on," he said.

Mary Lou shook her head and looked at Bill as if seeing him for the first time. Slowly she swung her legs out of the car and, clutching his arm, walked into the building that would be her temporary home for the next three months.

Inside the atmosphere was as dismal as the outside. Everything was painted institutional beige: a light brown and mustard. It seemed to be the color of choice for all public buildings. Perhaps because it looked the same when it was dirty as when it was clean. The carpet backing showed through in places where many feet had trod through the years. One picture hung on the wall. It was of a man with a handlebar mustache and clothing reminiscent of the turn of the century. Mary Lou wondered who he was: maybe Mr. Dunston, the original founder of the hospital.

Mrs. Dobins, the housemother, waddled into the room. Her small eyes, set too close together, gave her a suspicious look. Gray hair escaped from the bun loosely fastened to the back of her head. She frowned and looked sharply at Mary Lou.

"You were supposed to be here by five, young lady." She consulted a large over- sized watch that looked like it was cutting off the circulation on her wrist. "It's now after six. The others have all gone to supper." Her voice was low and grating.

"I'm not hungry," Mary Lou whispered. "It was snowing so hard and the traffic was heavy. It took longer than we expected." She knew her meager excuse was lost on this woman.

Bill picked up the luggage and stood, waiting for direction.

"They won't feed you now," Mrs. Dobins continued. "The patients work in the kitchen, you know. They're hard to manage when they're tired."

"I'll just go to my room and unpack," Mary Lou said trying not to look as miserable as she felt.

"What's your name?" the woman asked consulting a smudged list.

"Mary Louise Hammond."

"You're in room two-twelve with Kate Stephens."

Mary Lou breathed a sigh of relief. She and Kate had been roommates since the beginning of their training and were good friends. She knew she would need Kate's exuberance to get her through this rotation.

Bill shifted the weight of the suitcases ready to carry them upstairs.

Mrs. Dobins frowned. "This is as far as you go." She pointed to him with a fat finger. "No visitors allowed past the parlor."

"But I was just going to carry these upstairs. They're heavy." He gave her his most beguiling smile, showing deep dimples and a cleft in his chin.

"She can carry her own suitcases," Mrs. Dobins said, glaring at him.

He shrugged. "I guess I'd better go. I have some studying to do. Call me tomorrow night, okay?" He gave Mary Lou a quick kiss on the cheek as Mrs. Dobins looked on; her brows knit together, her lips pursed.

Mary Lou gave him a weak smile as she tucked a note in his pocket. Bill grinned back and walked out the door.

The notes were a game they had played since they started dating two years earlier. Mary Lou would write a note backwards. When Bill got home he would hold it up to a mirror and read it. The first time she had done it, he was confused.

"What's this, Egyptian hieroglyphics? My major is history, not ancient languages."

She laughed. "When I was a child I should have been left-handed, but Mother insisted I learn to do everything with my right hand. I had an especially hard time with writing."

She told Bill about her mirror-image writing and her pretend world. He had found her story touching. Growing up in a household with three sisters, he couldn't imagine the girl's loneliness. It became their secret. She wrote notes backwards and he read them in the mirror. They were usually funny and clever, and, they always ended with *Love you forever—M.L.*

Now he had to leave her in this place. Even he could feel the negative vibrations emanating from the entire complex. It felt as if all the tortured souls from decades past were crying out their anguish. He shivered, looked back one more time, and drove away.

Mary Lou stood at the door watching the car recede into the distance until it disappeared in the falling snow. The wind had picked up, blowing and drifting the heavy flakes. As she closed the door, shutting out the outside world, she had an uncontrollable urge to cry. "What a desolate place this is. Maybe it will look better in the daylight," she thought.

"All right, Hammond, get your suitcases up to your room. Don't want the floor cluttered up. Here's your key. One flight up and to your left."

"Thank you," she muttered. As she trudged up the dimly lit stairs lugging her cases, Mary Lou felt an almost overpowering heaviness around her. Wraiths from the past seemed to lurk in every corner. She hesitated for a moment trying to identify the strange sound. What was it?

"I will never last three months in this place," Mary Lou muttered continuing up the stairs. She had an unexplainable apprehension that, if she stayed that long she might never leave.

When she found her room, she fussed with the lock for a long time. When the bolt finally turned, the door pushed in with an eerie groan. She looked up at the ten-foot high ceiling. A single naked bulb hung from a cord in the center casting frightening shadows on the walls.

Mary Lou was glad she wasn't occupying the room alone. The sight of Kate's things strewn around gave it a familiar feeling. She went to the window where all she could see were swirling flakes of snow. A cold draft blew through the poorly fitting sash. The whistling wind sent a chill through her. She turned as she heard a familiar voice.

"Hi, Kiddo. I thought you'd never get here," Kate's throaty voice called from the doorway. Her plump, curvaceous body bounced into the room. Straight ash blond hair framed her round face in a pixie cut. "You missed supper. It wasn't much, but I stuck a buttered roll in my purse for you."

Kate held out her meager offering. Mary Lou took it, smiling at her friend. Maybe a few bites would make her feel better.

"You look awful," Kate said. "What's the matter, couldn't tear yourself away from Billy Boy?"

Mary Lou sat down on the bed. It gave a creak under her slight frame. "This place gives me the creeps. It's so depressing. And there are ghost-like shadows everywhere. I feel a terrible heaviness. Don't you?"

"Come on, Lulu, it'll be a new challenge, and it's only three months. You know how fast these rotations go. And, this is the last one. Then we take our State Boards and we'll be real registered nurses." Kate grabbed Mary Lou's hands and danced her around the room. Kate had that effect on everyone. She could take an uncomfortable situation and make it funny. Soon the girls fell on the bed laughing. To her, life was an adventure to be lived and enjoyed.

The girls had grown to be hard and fast friends, sharing everything with one another. When Kate decided that Mary Lou was too formal a name, she started calling her friend Lulu, and had done so ever since. While Mary Lou took life too seriously, Kate poked fun at everything.

As they began unpacking their things, memorabilia and small personal treasures appeared from the recesses of their baggage. Mary Lou felt better already. A small stuffed bear reminded her of her first date with Bill. She pulled out a picture of herself as a child with her mother, a thin-lipped woman with a grim expression on her face. She clung to the little girl almost fiercely. Even the photo showed her dominance.

Mary Lou stopped to think about her past. "Why had she never been close to her mother?" she asked herself. She wasn't sorry to leave home when she started nurse's training. Now she felt more detached from her than ever. She couldn't share any of these experiences with her. Mother was too fastidious.

Mary Lou remembered the time she fell and needed stitches. Her dad had taken care of everything. Mother said he liked *earthy things* and *earthy women*. Mary Lou wondered why he ever married her; how she let him get her pregnant. It was an *earthy act*, not at all dignified. That was it. Her mother was a lady, a dignified lady; she was never a mother.

"Hey Lulu, stop daydreaming," Kate said. "We're unpacking, remember?"

"Huh?" Mary Lou shook her head. "Okay." Carefully she unpacked a heavy Bavarian, diamond cut crystal prism. The light reflected from its many surfaces. She placed it on the windowsill where the light from the setting sun would shatter into its spectral colors, sending rays of red, yellow, green, blue and purple across the room. She loved the primary colors; they represented life: a life she was looking forward to. She had bought it with money she saved from babysitting. Her mother said she shouldn't waste money on such a useless bauble.

"What can you possibly want with that thing?" her mother had asked.

But Mary Lou was determined. "I earned the money and you said I could buy anything I want. And I want this." It was the first time she had disagreed with her mother and it felt good.

Then she unpacked her real treasure and placed it on her dresser: a wooden inlay music box smooth and cool to the touch. She wound the mechanism, opened the cover, and watched tiny figures rise up from the inside and dance round and round to the tune of the "Blue Danube Waltz".

This was the only gift her father had ever sent to her: a present for her tenth birthday. When she had opened the box, she stared at the figures, enthralled. She imagined herself dancing with a handsome prince somewhere in far off Germany.

Mary Lou's father had left when she was quite young, barely old enough to remember him. Her mother told her he was killed in Germany shortly after he sent her the music box. She never knew the circumstances of his death, nor of his life either.

Mrs. Hammond was notified that she was the beneficiary of a large insurance policy. She thought more kindly of him after that, but to Mary Lou he would always be the romantic figure in her left-handed world. She treasured that memory.

Chapter 2

Mary Lou opened her eyes, unsure of where she was. She looked around the unfamiliar room trying to get oriented. When she saw the bare light bulb hanging from the high ceiling, she remembered the car ride in the snow, and the menacing wrought iron fencing, the buildings looking like they were right out of a horror movie. She shuddered. She saw her prism on the windowsill and her music box on the dresser. They reminded her of home, but gave her little comfort. Then she thought of Bill. He felt so far away. When would she be able to see him again?

"Come on, Lulu, we'll be late for breakfast," Kate called nudging her with a foot. Mary Lou nodded, got out of bed, and headed for the communal bathroom down the hall. The chilly room held three shower stalls, four toilets, and the same number of sinks: most of them cracked and rust stained. The handles squeaked when she turned them. She didn't have time for a shower. She just splashed water on her face and brushed her teeth.

She looked in the unadorned mirror. God I look awful. Her dark curly hair insisted on doing its own thing. She attempted to brush it out, but the curls sprang back into an unruly mop. Dark smudges under her brown eyes attested to the restless night.

"Lulu," Kate called, her voice sounding impatient.

"Coming." Mary Lou threw her clothes on and was about to run after Kate when she felt for the silver chain that Bill had given her. It wasn't around her neck. She searched the bed and found it under the pillow. The loose clasp had come undone during the night. I've got to get this fixed, she promised herself for the umpteenth time. If I lose it, I'll never forgive myself. She fastened the chain around her neck, grabbed her coat and the heavy textbook they had bought, and then ran after Kate.

The snow crunched under their feet as they hurried to the building that housed the dining room. The sun had not yet put in its appearance and the waning moon cast a cold light on the snow.

"Brrr," Kate complained. "It's freezing out here." They walked faster as the wind crawled under their coats and wrapped itself around their legs reaching all the way up into their snuggies.

The girls stepped gingerly into a cheery room with flowered curtains covering the old windows. Tables were set for two or four diners. White tablecloths and napkins added a homey touch. It could have been a corner restaurant in a middle class neighborhood. The smell of pancakes and bacon filled the room.

"Come on, Lulu," Kate said pulling her along. "This is our table. They were assigned last night."

They sat at a table for two just as a middle-aged woman shuffled up to them. Without saying a word, she plopped down two glasses of orange juice, spilling a fair amount on the tablecloth.

"They're patients," Kate whispered. "The ones who aren't too sick help with the work. They wait on tables, work in the kitchen, and even bake bread and pies."

"Oh no," Mary Lou groaned. "There goes the waistline." After the traditional institutional food they had been eating for the past two years, the thought of home baked goods was tantalizing. This place might not be so bad after all, she thought.

"Java or cow?"

"Excuse me?" Mary Lou looked up at the woman glaring down at her. The black eyes stared at her with a look she had never seen before. Suddenly the strange look faded and was replaced by a vacant stare.

"Java or cow, coffee or milk, Java or cow, coffee or milk," she repeated over and over in a singsong fashion. After a moment she seemed to compose herself and stood at attention.

"I-I'll have coffee," Mary Lou said.

"Me too," Kate replied.

When the woman left the girls looked at each other. Kate shrugged. "That was weird. I suppose we'll get used to them, eventually."

After they had eaten their fill of pancakes, bacon, rolls and fresh coffee, they saw an imposing figure in white walk into the room. She was tall and slender with her faded blond hair pulled back in a bun. A nurse's cap with a stiff wing standing out on each side was perched on top of her head. It looked as if she might fly away at any moment.

No makeup adorned a stern face that might have been pretty at one time. The skirt of the shapeless uniform fell almost to her trim ankles. Her shoes were of the sturdy orthopedic variety that lasted forever.

"Ladies, attention please," she said in a voice both authoritative and impersonal. "My name is *Miss* Dillard. I will be in charge of your experience here at Hillside Mental Hospital. Come to me with any problems you might have."

She looked around the room. "I presume you have all finished your breakfast?"

"I don't think it matters if we're finished or not," Kate whispered shoving the last bite into her mouth.

The instructor's expression remained cool and aloof. "You will now follow me to classroom number one to begin your orientation."

Dutifully the girls followed dragging their coats, hats and books. They shivered as they marched inside the cold classroom. Someone had left a window open. Snow lined the sill and dripped steadily onto the floor leaving a damp stain down the wall and formed a puddle on the weathered wooden floor. Miss Dillard frowned as she closed the window and swept the snow into the wastebasket.

"Attention to the blackboard, please. These are your schedules for the next three months. You will spend the first two weeks in class from nine to four with a one-hour break for lunch. During this time you may wear street clothes. But when you work on the wards, you must be in uniform. That includes your caps." She looked around at the group as if expecting someone to disagree. "This afternoon I will take you on a short tour of parts of the facility. There are only certain wards on which you will obtain your psychiatric experience. You will not be allowed to enter the others.

"I have listed the various rotations on the board. Find your name and write them down. I expect you all to be responsible for your own schedules. This is a large institution and we have students from five nursing schools here at any one time. So don't ask for changes." Her steel-gray eyes studied each student.

Mary Lou felt them bore into her and shivered. You can bet your life that I won't ask for anything from you, she thought.

Miss Dillard's voice droned on. "To round out your experience here, you will spend time in Hydrotherapy, Electro-convulsive Therapy, and Insulin Coma Therapy. These are all proven methods for treating mental illness." Again she scanned the group.

"You will each spend one to two weeks on the open wards, in the Crib Room, on the Post-Lobotomy Ward, and on 13, which is women's violent. You are very fortunate to have the opportunity to spend time at this institution. Some of the cases here you are not likely to see anywhere else. I suggest you make the most of the experience." She stopped for a moment and, again, looked around. Her expression appeared to soften a bit.

"A word of caution. Many of these patients are dangerous. On the locked wards an attendant will accompany you at all times. Never turn your back on a patient. A few of the students have been injured. None seriously though. Are there any questions?"

Most of the girls were too stunned to say a word. Violence? Injury? They looked at each other with apprehension and fear.

"And, you will probably hear the legend of the ghost roaming the grounds. It doesn't exist." A deep furrow formed between her eyes. "All right then, proceed to the auditorium for your first lecture by Dr. Samuels on the history of mental illness."

The doctor's lecture proved to be disappointing. His voice droned on in a monotone. Undoubtedly he had given this lecture too often and didn't bother to vary his presentation. He seemed to want to finish as quickly as possible.

Mary Lou heard Kate letting out sighs of frustration and boredom.

Miss Dillard spoke about the history of the hospital. This information was interesting from an historical point of view, but most of the girls grew restless. They really didn't care that the wealthy Dunston family had created a trust to build and maintain this institution in 1871; after their daughter was diagnosed with a severe mental illness.

It might have been modern then, Mary Lou thought, but when she looked around, she saw age and deterioration everywhere.

Miss Dillard droned on, "When the trust was no longer able to maintain the hospital, the State assumed responsibility." She continued for another fifteen minutes. Then she turned the lecture over to the therapist, who briefly outlined her role in treating the patients. It didn't seem very impressive.

When they finally finished, the girls filed out and eagerly headed for the dining room.

"God they were boring," Kate moaned. "I almost fell asleep."

"I know," Mary Lou said. "I kept nudging you. Say, what did you think about that ghost thing?" She shivered as she said the words.

Kate grinned. "Like Dillard said, no such thing."

Chapter 3

After lunch the students lined up for a tour of the facility. Since the buildings were not connected to one another, everyone bundled up in heavy coats, scarves, and mittens. They shivered in the biting cold air, a Chicago cold: wind whipping around corners, sneaking under skirts, penetrating through skin and tissue to the very bone. In each building tiny particles of ice crusted along the bottoms of the windows. The patterns inched their way up the glass. Occasionally a face appeared, sometimes inquisitive, but more often it held the vacant stare of the mentally ill.

"This building houses both men and women in segregated wards. These patients are not violent. They could conceivably live in the community in sheltered circumstances, but the majority are homeless with no known family." Miss Dillard's voice penetrated the air as deeply as the cold.

The girls crowded through the door hoping to find some warmth. They wrinkled their noses at the musty rooms with crumbling plaster where the dampness had penetrated the building itself. Again all the walls wore a faded coat of institutional beige paint—not a decoration in sight.

A skinny crone ran up to the group, dancing around and waving her arms. Her hair straggled along sunken cheeks; her eyes clouded with age; her yellowish skin was deeply lined.

"See these hands?" she said grimacing. "They're nothing but bloody stumps." She twirled around three times, ran up to an old piano in a corner and began to play.

"Don't mind her," Miss Dillard said. "That's Josephine. She puts on an act for all the new students. She's harmless and some students find her entertaining."

"Oh I'm nothing but garbage," Josephine wailed as she began to crawl into a tall waste can. "Throw me away. Dump me along the side of the road. I'm worthless."

The instructor frowned, showing her displeasure. "That will be enough, Josephine. These are the new students and I expect you to be as helpful as possible."

"Yes Ma'am." The old woman grinned showing toothless gums then turned and stared directly at Mary Lou. She screwed up her face, sidled up to the girl, and whined. "I know something. I know everything. I know all about the ghost. Yes, I know who she is, where she walks. I know." She cackled, a grating sound, twirled around twice, and ran away.

Mary Lou shivered. What a creepy old witch, she thought.

The girls began murmuring as they watched the woman disappear around a corner.

"Pay no attention to Josephine," Miss Dillard said. "She likes to frighten the students with talk of ghosts. I have been here a long time and have had no direct experience with anything supernatural. Some imaginative people claim to have seen a white floating object in certain places, but I put no credence in these sightings."

Mary Lou stared at the instructor. Something in her tone didn't sound convincing.

They entered another ward where women walked aimlessly about while others sat and stared out the window. A woman in a nun's habit came up to them making the sign of the cross.

"Good morning, Miss Dillard, God bless you."

"I wonder if she's really a nun?" Mary Lou whispered.

As if she'd heard her Miss Dillard said. "Good morning, Sister."

As the patient walked away Miss Dillard turned to the students. "Sister Beatrice had a series of nervous collapses. It became impossible for her to continue living in the convent with the other nuns. She's been here for fifteen years."

Mary Lou felt sick at heart as she watched these hopeless people. Some were talking, but making little or no sense.

"A good many of these patients here have had pre-frontal lobototomies," Miss Dillard continued. Doctor Forester will be explaining that surgical procedure to you tomorrow. It consists of severing certain pathways to the brain to make the patient more tractable."

Many of the students looked at each other with disbelief in their eyes. Severing pathways to the brain? More tractable? What did it all mean?

Miss Dillard then led them to the men's ward. They watched a young man sitting quietly in a corner wiggling his fingers rhythmically. Suddenly a smile flashed across his face. He looked up at Miss Dillard and said, "Maybe I'll play again." Then he looked back at his fingers.

"He repeats the same thing over and over," she explained. "He was a promising young violinist from a prominent family. During a period of extreme stress, he developed uncontrollable schizophrenia. After the more conservative forms of treatment failed, the doctors performed a lobotomy." She shook her head and turned away as he smiled and repeated his litany.

"Maybe I'll play again. Do you think so?"

"Excuse me a moment," Miss Dillard said as she walked into another room. Mary Lou and Kate saw her talking to a man. His thin graying hair fell across his face. He stood with hunched shoulders staring at the wall. Miss Dillard put her arm protectively around his shoulder and flipped his hair out of his eyes.

"What's going on in there?" Kate whispered. "Old Dill Pickle looks almost human." Kate sidled up to the door for a closer look.

"You shouldn't call her that," Mary Lou whispered.

"Why not? Her face looks just like one."

"Kate, come away," Mary Lou cautioned. "If she sees that you watching her, there'll be hell to pay."

"Shush."

The girls both heard Miss Dillard's voice talking softly to the man. "Did you eat your breakfast, Ben?"

He mumbled something inaudible.

"I'll come and see you later."

They quickly moved back as their instructor returned. Her face, momentarily, appeared almost caring. She immediately replaced it with her mask of aloofness and led the way to another locked door.

As she opened it the girls smelled mostly disinfectants and mustiness. Patients sat in the day room: reading, playing cards, checkers, listening to radios. Their behaviors seemed almost normal.

A tall black man came up to the group and searched each face, then he looked down at Mary Lou and smiled. "You look just like my dead wife," he said with a lascivious gleam in his eye.

Her eyes widened with fear. She grabbed Kate's hand and shrank behind her roommate.

Miss Dillard ignored the remark. "Come girls, this way." She led them to a building across from the dining room. "This is the amusement hall. We have entertainment as often as possible. Movies every Friday night. You are welcome to come, if you like. The ambulatory patients with ground privileges may go on their own, but attendants must accompany the others. The movies are usually light comedy or animal adventure films, no violence nor anything too exciting. Some of the patients react inappropriately."

She looked at the students' faces. Then she continued.

"Various fraternal organizations sponsor dances regularly. We ask that you come to some of them and dance with the patients. They do enjoy it."

"I'll bet they do," Kate whispered. "Who wants these loonies pawing all over them? You never know where they put their hands." She shivered.

"Oh Kate." Mary Lou shook her head. "You always think the worst."

"It's true. Just watch them." She cocked her head to the side, and then wrinkled her nose as she watched a man playing with himself. "I am not dancing with any of them."

They walked outside to another building. The weather had softened a little as the sun melted some of the ice. Mary Lou wished she and Kate could go skating or walking, anywhere to get away from this depressing place.

"This is the therapy building," Miss Dillard said unlocking the door. She pointed to a section and explained without any emotion, as if she had repeated the words too many times. "Electroconvulsive Therapy and Insulin Coma Therapy are administered in here. We won't be observing them today. After you've had the theory behind the procedures, you will be assisting."

They walked into another area where moisture clung to the wall in droplets. It felt like a sauna. "This is the Hydrotherapy Department. Water has been used as a therapeutic agent for centuries. Warm water has a sedative effect; cold water for stimulation."

A row of shower stalls lined the wall. A naked woman stood in each stall as attendants, clad in rubber boots and aprons, sprayed cold water over their bodies. Their skin glowed a peculiar pink color. The cold water shocked even the most withdrawn into some sort of awareness.

"What are they doing?" one of the students asked, her eyes wide and frightened.

"This is the salt glow. It works for severely depressed patients. Their bodies are rubbed with a coarse salt. The friction of the rub dilates the blood vessels to the skin giving them that rosy glow. The effect is stimulating. After the treatment they undergo group psycho-therapy." She sighed and shook her head.

"Unfortunately, most revert to their previous states. But, if we can help even one of these withdrawn patients, we're making progress." Martha Dillard didn't sound as if she believed her own words.

"It looks like torture from the Middle Ages if you ask me," Kate whispered.

"You will all have an opportunity to experience this therapy first hand," their instructor continued. "You will perform these treatments on each other before you treat patients."

A groan went up throughout the group. Mary Lou shivered at the thought of icy water spraying on her salted skin.

"Keep you voices down in here," Miss Dillard said. "One patient is receiving the cold wet sheet wrap. Look in the window without disturbing the procedure, please."

Two burly attendants forced a terrified woman down onto a cot.

"This is a form of sedation," Miss Dillard explained. "The patient lays on the cot and is wrapped, mummy style, in cold wet sheets."

When her naked body felt the cold sheet, the woman screamed and let fly a string of obscenities. "You bitches. Let me go or I'll bite your boobs off!"

"Shut up!" one of the attendants shouted, "or I'll break your arm."

The woman groaned and thrashed as the attendants deftly wrapped the sheets around her body finally rendering her helpless. She continued to scream and curse. Miss Dillard frowned. Mary Lou trembled as she grabbed Kate's arm to steady herself. Kate grimaced and turned away.

After a few moments the patient began to relax. The attendants placed blankets over the wet sheets and, soon, the woman was asleep.

"As you can see," Miss Dillard said, "this is a form of both restrain and sedation. Occasionally we get a patient who panics and must be released from the sheets, but the majority goes to sleep. You will wrap each other to experience the treatment."

"Not me," Kate muttered. "I get claustrophobic. I'll die in there."

"You won't die, Kate. Don't be so melodramatic," Mary Lou said.

As they walked away from the area, Mary Lou said. "Oh God, Kate, those poor people. How can they go on living?"

"It's pretty awful, Lulu, but they don't seem to have much choice. Cheer up, two days down, eighty-eight more to go."

"I'll never make it," Mary Lou said, dragging her feet.

"Oh yes you will," Miss Dillard said obviously overhearing the girls. "They all do. Then you'll leave us and go back to the real world. Most of you will forget us. A few will remember."

Mary Lou felt a wave of pity for the woman. She seemed so hard and business-like, but maybe she's hiding some secret, deep inside her. Why did she stay in this awful place?

"How long have you been here, Miss Dillard," Mary Lou asked timidly.

The woman looked away, her face softening for just a moment. Then she turned to the girls. "Too long."

The instructor turned her attention to the class. "I won't take you to the more disturbing wards today. That will come later. You'll all spent time in the Crib Room and on 13, the women's violent ward. This is as much as most of you can absorb right now. Come, back to the classroom."

Chapter 4

The students spent the next two weeks in the classroom, their evenings completely taken up with studying. The food was much better quality than they were used to. They stuffed themselves with tasty entrees, homemade bread and bakery goods. Waistlines began to bulge.

"Kate, this is disgraceful. I can't button my skirt. This gorging has got to stop," Mary Lou moaned.

"But it's all so good," Kate said. She thought for a minute then screwed up her face. "Maybe we can compromise: no second helpings and regular outdoor exercise. All we've been doing is sitting these last two weeks. If we're not in class, we're in this room, hitting the books."

"That's a good idea," Mary Lou said. "In fact, let's go out right now and measure out a course where we can run, or, at least, walk fast."

The mid-December day was unseasonably mild. A harsh late afternoon light lay over the complex of buildings. The snow had packed hard after a freeze the previous week making walking easy. A soft breeze blew from the southeast.

"Boy, it's nice out here," Kate said.

"Don't let it fool you," Mary Lou said. "This is Chicago. You can't trust the weather. You know that. You've lived here all your life. Tomorrow it could be in the teens or even lower. We'd better bundle up."

The girls began a slow jog around the buildings. They passed the chapel, a small building that held nondenominational Sun- day services. The bakery lay to their right. The smell of fresh bread wafted on the air doubling their determination to exercise. Ahead the cottage wards looked almost like a run down suburban area. The original plan was to provide a home-like setting where patients could live in a family atmosphere instead of a large impersonal institution, but buildings were sadly overcrowded. They saw faces staring at them from the curtained windows. Most of them just stared, but a few disembodied hands appeared and waved slowly back and forth. They turned left at the pharmacy to a large open space behind the power plant.

"I wonder what's down that way?" Mary Lou said. "It looks like a fence. See, way down at the end." She pointed to wooden posts poking out of the snow. "Let's find out."

They ran the distance, but were breathing hard when they reached the fence.

"Boy," Kate said blowing hard, "am I out of shape." She leaned against the old rotting wood standing out at odd angles; in some places new posts replaced the old ones.

"Wow, it looks like a cemetery," Mary Lou said. "See there where the snow's melted? It's a grave marker."

"Are you sure? Let's climb over." Kate already had one leg over the low railing.

"No, we'll get in trouble. Here I can reach my hand through. There, see where I've wiped the snow away?" She squinted at the faded markings. "It says Robert Gil—something. I can't make it out, but the date is pretty clear. My God! It says 1848 to 1913. I wonder who all these people were."

"I don't know, but it's kind of spooky." Kate looked around. "Do you think there really is a ghost around here?"

Mary Lou shivered. "If there is, this is the place it would be lurking after dark. Let's go back. I don't want to be anywhere near here when the sun sets."

At that moment an animal ran behind the cemetery fence. It turned and glared at them with yellow eyes.

"What was that?" Mary Lou said gripping a post.

"I don't know," Kate answered. "It looked like some kind of strange cat, but it's awfully big."

As Mary Lou looked around, the cat had disappeared, but she thought she saw someone slip behind a large oak tree. She froze. "I think someone's behind that tree."

Kate turned. "No, you're imagination's playing tricks on you, but let's get out of here, right now."

The girls ran without looking back, but Mary Lou could feel unfriendly eyes watching them. She tripped and fell over a mound of snow. When she tried to get up, her limbs refused to move. She saw that the light was just beginning to fade. Would someone or something grab her at any minute? She turned and thought she saw a figure blending in with the shadows of the trees. Was it the ghost or someone human? Scrambling to her feet, she hurried to catch up with Kate as they reached the shelter of the buildings. In the distance they heard a peculiar howl. It wasn't the wind. Was it the animal they had seen? Or was it something else?

They were both breathing hard. "Someone was out there," Mary Lou gasped. "I could feel it. Someone who didn't want us at that cemetery and that strange howling."

"It was probably that animal," Kate said with little conviction in her voice. "Come on, forget about it. Let's go to the dining room. It must be time for supper. I'm starved."

Chapter 5

"So, now that the first two weeks are over, what's the verdict?" Bill asked. They sat in a small restaurant near the hospital, their first date since the rotation started. "Think you'll make it?" He took Mary Lou's hand and gave it a squeeze. His smile usually sent warmth through her, but tonight, for some reason, it looked forced.

"It's such a sad place," she said shaking her head. "The people are so pitiful. There's simply no hope for most of them." She gave a deep sigh, picked up a piece of fried chicken, took a small bite, and then put it down again.

She sat back and told him about the tour of the facility. She noted Bill's grimace as she described the colorless wards, the hopeless existence of the patients.

"Geesh," he said pushing his plate away. "I'm glad I'm not spending time there. That's a living death." He gave a small shudder then smiled at her.

"Let's talk about something else. I got my assignment for my term paper in history. I've decided to do it on early Chicago. I'm going to concentrate on the reconstruction period after the Chicago fire."

Mary Lou scratched her head and gave him a puzzled look. "I don't even know when the Chicago fire happened. I was never really interested in history."

"Shame on you," he said giving her a stern look. "Let me give you a lesson. The year was 1871. There had been a terrible drought over the whole Midwest. Since most of the buildings then were made of wood, they were always catching fire." Bill rambled on about the story of the O'Leary's cow and how the fire spread quickly through the old wooden structures.

At that moment the waitress came over to the table. "More coffee?" She gave Bill an engaging smile.

"Sure. How about it, Mary Lou?"

"I guess so." For some reason she felt far removed from Bill tonight. She couldn't concentrate on what he was saying. Her thoughts kept returning to Hillside and its inhabitants.

"Now, where was I?" Bill continued. "Oh, with the strong wind that was blowing that night, it took only an hour for the fire to spread all the way to the middle of the city...."

Bill kept talking oblivious to her inattention. Mary Lou watched his lips opening and closing, his hand movements emphasizing his story, but his words didn't register on her brain.

He took a swallow of coffee, his eyes animated with the subject. "Can you imagine what that was like?"

She shook his head. "Not really." What had he just said? She didn't know, but he was so engrossed in his subject that he paid little attention to her.

"Over two hundred people died and just as many were missing. Over three square miles were completely destroyed, the entire business district—gone." He slashed his hand across the table as if wiping out everything.

"It was ironic that the O'Leary's house was still standing. Isn't that ironic?"

Mary Lou screwed up her face and gave her head a shake as if she were coming out of a dream. "How can you remember all those facts?"

Bill shrugged. "I love history. All this research makes it come alive. It's all so interesting. I drove to the area where the O'Leary's house stood and just walked around. I could almost see it happening: horse-drawn fire trucks, bells clanging, the bucket brigade, people screaming, running, trampling each other." His eyes shone with excitement. He made history come to life.

"You'll make a great professor some day," she said. She knew that was his goal and he would certainly succeed.

When Bill finally finished, Mary Lou was relieved. She realized that he was so involved in his own life and interests, that he wasn't at all sympathetic to her needs.

"Was there anything left?" she asked. She had to show some interest in the conversation or he would be angry.

"The old Water Tower was the only building left on Michigan Avenue. The stockyards were okay. But people started to rebuild right away. You can't keep good people down, and Chicagoans are great people." He grinned.

"Would you like some dessert?" the waitress asked coming a little too close to Bill.

He looked her up and down. "What do you suggest?"

Mary Lou bristled at the implication.

"The apple pie is great tonight."

"Sold," he said. "You want some, Hon?"

"No thank you."

"What's wrong?" Bill asked after the girl had left. "You're getting your hackles up."

"I saw the way you looked at her. Do you have to flirt with every female that comes your way?"

"Hey, wait a minute. I can look, can't I?" He frowned and shook his head. "You're in a lousy mood tonight. I'll blame it on Hillside. But I'm under a lot of stress, too. Don't push me."

Bill ate his pie in silence. Mary Lou played with her napkin. Suddenly she wanted to be out of the restaurant, back to Hillside, walking. What's wrong with me? She wondered. I've been so morbid lately. I can't help thinking about all those people buried in that cemetery.

As they drove back, Mary Lou took Bill's hand. "I'm sorry. Let's not argue about silly things. Kate and I walked around the place and found an old cemetery. I've been thinking about it ever since." She didn't tell him that she felt sure that someone was watching them nor the strange howling sound. After all, it could have been her imagination and the sound just an animal.

At the stoplight Bill turned and gave her a peck on the nose. "All's forgotten, but you'd better stay away from that cemetery. There might be ghosts lurking about."

He deliberately exaggerated the words in fun, but Mary Lou felt a chill run up her spine.

When they reached the gate, Bill said, "I can feel the heaviness around here. Try and stay cheerful, will ya? And stay away from that cemetery, promise?"

"Okay." They kissed goodnight and Mary Lou walked into the nurses' residence. Before she closed the door, she looked back and waved to him.

For a long time she stood in the parlor, feeling something or someone pulling at her. She had to walk, to think, to clear her mind. Bill had annoyed her, flirting with the waitress. He flirted with Kate all the time, but that didn't seem to bother her. Why should she let it upset her? She was beginning to wonder if Bill really cared for her. And, what were her real feelings toward him?

Without realizing it she went out and walked outside along the edge of the buildings. The round cold disk of a full moon shed its frigid light over the desolate ground. Unkempt faces peered from dirty windows; windows framed with ice crystals climbing up the glass as if nature was attempting to provide a meager decoration. Vacant stares gazed unseeing, unknowing, until the chill drove them away. Before she realized where she was, she saw the fence surrounding the cemetery.

"What am I doing here? Am I getting as loony as some of these patients?" she said aloud. She stood at the fence for a long time staring at the isolated grave markers showing through the blanket of snow. Wispy clouds crept across the face of the brazen moon, covering its nakedness. Soon the icy light disappeared behind a dark cloud.

Mary Lou remembered the words Bill said jokingly; she remembered Josephine talking about the ghost; she remembered the silent figure hiding behind the tree and the strange animal roaming about. There's something out here, I know it, she thought. An adrenaline rush propelled her toward the lighted buildings, but they held no welcoming warmth, only ignorance, desolation and hopelessness.

Chapter 6

The next night the girls spent the evening studying. It was late and Kate had fallen asleep. Mary Lou felt lightheaded and somewhat detached. Various psychiatric diagnoses floated through her mind: schizophrenia, dementia, hysteria, and tertiary syphilis. She had to put the books down. She picked up a pencil, put it in her left hand, and began writing a letter to Bill in mirror image.

Dear Bill,
I'm working so hard that I feel
this will never end. This is a different
world. I hope I can last the three
months. I'm going to try, real hard.
    Love you,
    Mary Lou

Then, as if guided by an unseen hand, she scribbled something else at the bottom of the page. Without rereading the note, she folded it and put it aside. Overcome with exhaustion, she slid down in bed, books, papers, and pencils toppling to the floor. She drifted into a dream-filled sleep.

A Victorian mansion with a horse-drawn carriage pulling up to the entrance...Bits of conversation...someone mentioned a porte cochere. A wealthy woman being assisted from the carriage, scolding the driver—a butler—something about guests—from The Friends of the Opera. She heard the name Mrs. Montague. A woman sitting at the dressing table calling to a man named Samuel. Something about money—overdrawn account—cutting him off. Accusing him of having an affair—a heated argument....

"So what's this strange dream you had?" Bill asked. "You sound so shaky."

Mary Lou gripped the phone, her knuckles turning white. "It was the weirdest thing, like I was watching a movie. Like it wasn't happening to me, but to other people."

"There's no accounting for dreams," Bill said. "It's probably something your subconscious dredged up. You said you were studying, you were tired, a jumble of facts in your head. The subconscious plays it out in a dream, that's all."

"But I saw a porte cochere. I remember hearing the words. I don't even know what that means."

"It's a passageway from the street to a courtyard," Bill explained.

"But how can I dream of something I never heard of? Don't you think my dreams would have something to do with mental illness? With these poor unhappy people? Instead I dream about some rich woman from the turn of the century." Mary Lou felt more confused by the minute.

"How do you know it was the turn of the century?" Bill asked.

"I guess by the clothes, the horse-drawn carriage, the house. I really don't know."

"Stop making a mountain out of a mole hill. I was telling you about the Chicago fire. Maybe that's what triggered it. By the way, you didn't leave a note in my pocket the other night," he scolded. "You're slipping."

"I know. I found it on the floor this morning. Stuck it in an envelope and mailed it. I'm getting so absent-minded.

"Oh, another thing. I have to get my silver chain fixed. It was on the floor again this morning. It came loose during the night and I sure don't want to lose it."

"Okay. Give it to me next Sunday and I'll take it to the jeweler and have a new clasp put on. Now forget about the dream. It doesn't mean anything. I'll talk to you tomorrow. Love you."

She heard the words, but they sounded empty. "Love you, too," she said by rote, but without emotion. "Bye."

As she walked back to her room, Mary Lou felt a sudden chill. That's what I get for roaming around outside in the cold. She felt as though someone was behind her. She turned abruptly half expecting to see the ghost, but there was nothing, only the dimly lit empty hallway.

I'm getting the creeps, she told her- self. There's no ghost. It's just talk to scare us. Better get down to work. The following day Dr. Forester was scheduled to talk about Electroconvulsive Therapy. Better be sure to get the name right. It'll certainly be on a test. Now, to finish the chapter. She walked into her room, opened the book and sat in the wooden chair at the small desk and began to read.

But she couldn't concentrate. Why do I talk to myself all the time, she wondered. For some reason it was comforting. She remembered her childhood, talking to the left-handed child in the mirror. How silly. But she had been so lonely. Mother said she should be satisfied to play with her dolls and coloring books. Other children made noise and messed the house. They gave Mother a headache. The mirror seemed the only place where Mary Lou had found a playmate. Someday I'll talk with a psychiatrist, she thought, and find out why I'm so bizarre.

She looked at her music box, smiled and wound it. She watched the tiny dancers and listened to the "Blue Danube Waltz". It was the only thing that gave her some comfort in this lonely place.

The following morning dawned to an overcast sky. Low hanging clouds blocked out the sun, one of those mid-winter days that never actually see light. Mary Lou had a fitful night filled with dreams that she didn't remember. She found her silver chain on the floor again.

"I'm not going to wear this until it's fixed," she muttered putting it in her jewelry box.

"What are you whispering about?" Kate asked. "Come on, I need some breakfast. We have to fortify ourselves. I hear that Dr. Forester is long winded."

As the girls hurried to the dining room, the wind whipped mercilessly at their faces. It was only a short distance, but they were half-frozen when they stomped through the door and made their way to their table.

"Java or cow, java or cow," Sarah, their waitress, mumbled rocking from one foot to the other.

"Java, we need lots of Java this morning," Kate said rubbing her hands together. She looked across the table at her roommate. "Are we going shopping Saturday? It's only a few weeks 'till Christmas."

"Gosh, I don't have much money. I'll have to get something for my mother and Bill, and you, of course." She knit her brows in a worried frown.

"I'm kind of broke, too," Kate said. "Tell you what, let's not buy each other anything this year. We'll go out to dinner when we need a lift, someplace nice. That will be our gift to ourselves." She sat back, looking pleased with her suggestion.

"Sounds good," Mary Lou agreed. "I never did like Christmas shopping anyway. It always makes me sad." The holidays at her house were sterile. Her mother went through the motions, but without any real joy. She looked down at the plate of bacon and eggs Sarah sat before her.

"What's wrong with you, Lulu? You look like you lost your best friend. I'm here, see?" Kate made a weird face and soon Mary Lou began laughing.

"Dig in," Kate said buttering a slice of warm toast. "Dr. Forester awaits."

The auditorium overflowed. Students and visiting professionals waited to hear the noted authority in the field of mental health.

"Be sure to take good notes," Mary Lou whispered to Kate. "Some exam is sure to cover this."

Kate nodded as she opened her notebook.

A tall regal-looking man stepped up to the podium. His piercing blue eyes looked over his audience. A shock of gray hair hung down over his high forehead. A pencil thin mustache adorned his upper lip. For a moment he rubbed a large hand over his prominent chin, then began to speak in a loud clear voice.

"Ladies and gentlemen, I am here today to discuss the modern treatment of mental illness. We must be aware that this problem has existed from time immemorial. Evidence shows us that mental disease goes back to primitive man. These societies surrounded themselves with magic and rituals. Harmful spirits and devils were suspected of causing some of the symptoms we see today. Archeologists have found many skulls with burr holes to let the evil spirits escape. Among the ancient Egyptians...."

His deep voice continued as he described in detail the procedures done in ancient times. Mary Lou looked around and saw fellow students scribbling as fast as they could.

"Interpretation of dreams went back to biblical times. Joseph's explanation of the Pharaoh's dream of the seven fat cows and the seven lean ones foretold seven years of plenty followed by the same number of famine years. So Freud wasn't the first to put credence in dreams...."

Mary Lou frowned. What about her dreams? What did they mean? Did she really want to know?

Dr. Forester's voice filled the hall, keeping his audience spellbound. "The standard treatment today for depression and schizophrenia is Electroconvulsive Therapy. Some of you may have already observed this treatment. It isn't as barbaric as it seems. Lay people refer to it as electroshock treatment or simply as shock treatments. These are misnomers. The patient does *not* experience a shock. After electrodes are applied to both temples, a small current passes through the brain. At that point consciousness is lost and, after a few seconds, a grand mal seizure is experienced." Again he looked over the audience. Some of them squirmed in their seats.

"After the patients regain consciousness, their minds remain clouded for fifteen to thirty minutes. Sometimes they experience headaches and nausea, but these symptoms are temporary. They have no memory of the procedure. We have found that depression is markedly improved after three or four treatments. Acute Schizophrenia responds to this treatment, but chronic cases have a poor outcome. Are there any questions so far?" He looked up, eyebrows raised, as if daring anyone to speak.

"Dr. Forester," a young man stood up. His trim figure looked attractive in the white shirt and pants the residents wore. "If the patients have no memory of the treatments, why are they so frightened of the procedure?"

"Good question. We feel they are afraid of the period immediately following the treatment when they awaken not knowing who they are or where they are. But, this amnesia passes in a very short time. Any other questions?" Again he looked over his audience. "Then we'll continue."

Mary Lou watched the young doctor sit down, a frown on his face, obviously not satisfied with the answer.

"The next form of therapy we will discuss this morning is Insulin Coma Therapy. Again, this is commonly referred to as Insulin Shock." He shook his head. "Not so. Some practitioners noticed that schizophrenics who lapsed into coma, for whatever reason, seemed to improve. In 1936 two forward thinking doctors began treating them with Insulin.

"We know that if insulin is injected into a fasting patient, his blood sugar will drop and he will become hypoglycemic. Enough Insulin will result in coma. The dosage is small at first, increasing in increments daily. The pre-coma phase is characterized by dizziness, somnolence,...."

Dr. Forester then described the stages that followed. His voice was mesmerizing and, for a moment, Mary Lou felt detached, as if she were somewhere else. She gave a slight shake of her head, blinked, and turned her attention back to the speaker.

"The treatment is terminated by administering glucose solution through a nasal tube feeding. We have found this effective in treating schizophrenics who do not respond to Electroconvulsive Therapy."

"Dr. Forester," the same young doctor called out. "Isn't this dangerous? What if the coma is allowed to go too far and becomes irreversible?"

The speaker frowned, obviously irritated by the question. "The patients are closely watched, young man. Rarely does this happen."

"How often is rarely?" the questioner continued.

"Infrequently, doctor, infrequently." He looked at his watch. "Our time is running out so there will be no more questions." His stern look at the audience told them that he meant it. The young doctor shook his head as he sat down.

"Next I will discuss a form of psychosurgery called Prefrontal Lobotomy. The procedure severs certain nerve fibers connecting parts of the brain. The purpose is to permanently alter behavior. This surgery eliminates aggressive and violent behavior in patients who cannot be controlled in any other way."

"Then they become the zombies we saw on the wards," Kate whispered.

"Some of these patients can return to society," Dr. Forester continued, "but they require a controlled environment. Most become like children for the rest of their lives."

"Dr. Forester, don't we have moral and ethical responsibilities with such drastic procedures?" The daring young doctor spoke again.

"Young man, we are not here to discuss ethics and morals," Dr. Forester answered, an angry tone to his voice. "We are talking about madness. Someday there will be medications to control and alter behavior. Today we have none. We use whatever methods work. And these, that I have just discussed, are *state of the art.*"

Dr. Forester folded his notes and marched off the stage. The audience applauded, but the young doctor looked annoyed as he turned and spoke to one of his colleagues, as if his questions had not been answered to his satisfaction.

"He's got guts," Kate said looking at the handsome young man with admiration. "I'll bet he'll never use these *state of the art* treatments of medieval torture."

They saw him conversing with a fellow doctor. His blond hair fell across his face as he vehemently shook his head. He reached up his hand and brushed it aside. At that moment he looked up and noticed the girls watching him. He smiled and waved at them.

Mary Lou felt her face flush and immediately looked down at the floor, but Kate smiled back.

"Come on," Mary Lou said, "let's go."

They joined their classmates leaving the auditorium, but Mary Lou couldn't get the face of the bold young doctor out of her mind.

Chapter 7

The following morning Miss Dillard called the students together. "Ladies, today some of you will witness Electroconvulsive Therapy. Ten of you will come with me. The rest of you will wait and go with Miss Parker. Too many students are distracting to the patients."

Kate looked at Mary Lou, grimaced and shrugged her shoulders. She was selected to go with the second group.

"This is scary, isn't it?" a diminutive blond mumbled to Mary Lou.

"It sure is." Mary Lou felt a chill creeping up her spine as she remembered Dr. Forester's words.

Miss Dillard led them into a dark cold room. They lined up around the periphery with strict instructions to remain silent. They were in no way to interfere with the therapy.

In a few moments an attendant rolled in a gurney with a wide-eyed young woman strapped to it. She thrashed her head from side to side, and then looked around, apparently recognizing the room.

"No! No!" she screamed, struggling to escape. Four strong arms lifted her writhing body from the gurney and placed her roughly on a table in the center of the room. The woman moaned and whined as the attendants quickly restrained her: a strap across her waist, leather restraints on her wrists, and a thick band to hold her head in place.

A nurse applied a gooey electrode paste to the woman's temples; another shoved a padded tongue blade between her teeth to muttered protestations.

Then a doctor in a white coat materialized in the gloom. He clamped a paddle into the paste on either side of the woman's head. Her eyed bulged in terror. Her teeth clamped down on the tongue blade. The doctor pushed a lever with his foot producing a slight humming sound. The woman on the table stiffened; her eyes rolled back in her head; her spine arched; her breathing stopped. A wet stain on the sheet and the smell of freshly voided urine made Mary Lou's stomach lurch. The woman's body began to convulse. At this point the nurses held her arms and legs to prevent injury while the doctor held her head.

Her skin had taken on a dusky hue when she finally took a deep snorting breath. As she exhaled, saliva bubbled around the tongue blade and slid down her chin. The convulsion lasted a full minute. To Mary Lou it seemed like an hour. The patient's limbs then relaxed as her breathing returned to normal. She remained in a stuporous state: saliva pooling in the grooves of her neck, perspiration staining the armpits of her gown, urine soaking the sheet. The attendants removed the restraints and placed her once more on the gurney and wheeled her out.

A classmate grabbed Mary Lou's arm and cringed against her letting out a small moan. That poor wretch had been striped of all remnants of dignity. Miss Dillard had told them that the patient would sleep for two to three hours. When she woke, she would be confused and suffer some memory lapses. Later a psychiatrist would talk to her and attempt to bring her back in touch with reality.

Mary Lou thought of the rest of her training. It was progressive: the sterile surgery with new procedures performed by brilliant young surgeons; the new antibiotics curing infections that had killed thousands in the past; sophisticated diagnostic procedures pinpointing the causes of diseases. But these treatments were comparable to the Dark Ages. There seemed to be no progress here. These were the forgotten ones. No one wanted them and no one seemed to care.

An attendant washed the table and someone wheeled in the next patient. The process began again, but this woman was stuporous to begin with. She didn't seem to be aware of what was happening to her.

"Hey Lulu, you're pale as a ghost," Kate said. "You're not eating your lunch."

Mary Lou pushed a potato from one end of her plate to the other. She couldn't swallow anything. She kept seeing the terror in the woman's eyes, hearing the buzzing of the machine, visualizing the seizure. She grimaced. "I don't feel well. That therapy was awful. I hope I don't have to watch anything like that again. You weren't even there with me." She gave Kate an accusing look as if she had chosen to go with the second group.

Kate shook her head. "Sorry, I didn't enjoy it either. But, as Dr. Forester said, it's an accepted form of treatment." She eyed Mary Lou's full plate.

"You'd better wrap up that stuff and take it with you. You know how mad Sarah gets if we leave food. She's liable to refuse to feed us, and tonight's fresh pie night."

Mary Lou marveled at how Kate could always think of her stomach. She made a sandwich, wrapped it in a napkin, and slipped it into her purse.

"Time for class," Kate chirped jumping out of her chair.

Mary Lou looked with envy at her roommate, always cheerful. This place didn't seem to phase her one bit. She simply took everything in stride.

After class the girls took their walk. It had become a routine, fifteen minutes each way to the cemetery and back. They walked briskly: partly because of the cold and because darkness came early in December. At the fence Mary Lou looked wistfully at the desolate surroundings. The snow had drifted leaving more grave markers exposed.

"Kate, look over there, in the corner near the oak tree." She pointed to something white jutting out of the snow. "What is it?"

The girls ran to the tree and stared at a tiny cross with a few fresh flowers laid across what appeared to be a pitifully small grave. No marker told the sad story of who or what was buried there.

"Someone put flowers on this grave," Mary Lou said. "I can hardly believe that. Who would bring flowers to an unmarked grave out here in the middle of winter?"

"It's so small," Kate said. "Look, it's right here in the corner. You can reach a hand in through the fence." She easily slid her hand through the wooden slats and touched the tiny cross.

"Maybe it's a pet," Mary Lou said, "a dog or a cat that lived on the grounds. Then, when it died, one of the caretakers buried it out here."

Kate frowned. "Could be, but who would put flowers on the grave?" She opened her eyes wide and made her mouth into an O. "Another mystery in the Hillside cemetery, first the ghost and now the flowers. Let's watch and see who comes out here."

"You're talking ridiculous," Mary Lou said looking around. "There's no way we can watch this cemetery. A short walk here in the afternoon isn't going to show us anything. We're in class and on the wards all day."

Kate shrugged. "Anyway, whenever either one of us is at a window facing the cemetery, we'll look out and see if anyone's walking this way. Okay?"

"I suppose. Now let's go back. I'm freezing." She turned around as the chill wind ran up her legs. "I always get the feeling that someone is watching us."

They turned and ran back, occasionally looking behind them. Mary Lou thought she saw the dark shape of an animal. Was it the same one they had seen before? Was it real or was it...?

Chapter 8

"Hammond, phone call," a voice called from the hallway.

"Go on, it's probably Billy Boy," Kate teased.

Mary Lou hurried to the phone. She was always eager to talk to Bill. He was her only link with the real world.

"Hi Hon," his cheery voice sounded over the wire. "How's my little joker tonight?"

"Hi Bill, I'm okay, but why are you calling me that?"

"That note you sent me. It wasn't the usual thing, you know. You sounded de- pressed and that last sentence was a dilly. It doesn't even look like your handwriting."

"What last sentence? What are you talking about?"

"Don't you remember what you wrote? Here let me read it to you.

Dear Bill,
I'm working so hard that I feel
this will never end. This is a different
world. I hope I can last the three
months. I'm going to try, real hard.
*   Love you,*
*   Mary Lou*

"Then you left a space and wrote this:

Help me! I died here in 1911.
Free me from this earthly prison.
Margaret Montague

"So, what's it all about?" Bill asked.

Mary Lou couldn't understand what he was saying. "What do you mean?"

"Just what I said." He repeated the message.

"I—I haven't the slightest idea," she answered, her mind suddenly confused. "I don't know anything about it, don't remember writing anything like that." She put a fist over her mouth and bit down on her knuckles.

"Don't get upset," Bill said in a soothing voice. "What were you doing when you wrote the note?"

Mary Lou screwed up her face and frowned, trying to remember. "I was studying. It was late and I was tired. I remembered that I had forgotten to give you a note, so I wrote it and put it aside. Then I went to sleep. I don't even remember what I wrote." Chills ran up her arms as she struggled to comprehend the strange words of the note.

"Then the message probably came from your subconscious mind," he said in a matter of fact tone. "Have you been read- ing a Victorian novel? Margaret Montague, 1911?"

"Novel, who has time for novels? I've been reading about psychoses, fragmented personalities, Electroconvulsive Therapy...." Her voice rose with each word.

"Easy, Honey, easy." Bill's soothing tone calmed her a little. "Maybe it was about that dream you had. Let's just forget it, okay?

Don't get all upset. Let me ask you one more question. You said that you and Kate take a walk every day to the old cemetery. Have you ever read any names and dates on the markers?"

"No, the gate's locked. We can't get inside. The markers close to the fence are so worn you can't read anything." She suddenly felt overwhelmed. "Oh Bill, I'm getting fragmented, disassociated, schizophrenic."

"Stop it," he commanded. "It's simply exhaustion and an overactive imagination. My suggestion is that you get some rest. Proofread any notes that you write. I'm sure it won't happen again."

"Okay. I'll ask Kate to watch for any strange behavior on my part. I think I am over tired. I'm going to bed now. Bye." After she hung up the phone she realized neither of them had said *I love you*. She shook her head, shuffled back to her room, threw herself on the bed, and stared at the ceiling thinking of the note. Did I really write such a thing without being aware of what I was doing? God, what's happening to me? She tossed and turned for a long time before she finally fell asleep.

After Bill hung up the phone, he thought long and hard. Mary Lou had been acting peculiar lately. He remembered her telling him of the strange dream of the Victorian mansion, the apparently wealthy woman.... I hope she's all right, he thought. I hope that place isn't getting to her. I think I'll ask Kate. Maybe she knows what the problem is.

Chapter 9

The following day Mary Lou and Kate decided to spend their free hour in the library doing research for their term papers.

"Look," Kate said pointing to a familiar figure curled in a corner. "Isn't that Josephine? What's she doing here? Let's go talk to her."

They walked over and looked down at the scrawny woman. "Hi Josephine," Kate said. "How are you?"

"I don't feel well," the woman whined. "I'm sick and I'm going to die at two o'clock this afternoon." She wrapped her arms around her frail body and rocked back and forth. Her lank greasy hair hung over her face obscuring her eyes.

"How do you know that?" Kate asked.

She pushed her hair aside, looked up, and squinted at the girls, a cunning smile crossing her face. "I know everything around here," she said. "Just ask me."

Mary Lou and Kate exchanged glances. Then Kate asked, "How do fresh flowers get in the cemetery?"

"Someone puts them there," the woman answered, grinning. Her toothless gums reminded Mary Lou of a fish.

"Who?" Kate prodded.

Josephine cackled. "That's the question, isn't it? Only I know the answer." With that she uncurled her lithe body, jumped up and began dancing around.

"Stop that, you'll get us thrown out of the library," Mary Lou said trying to grab the woman's arm. But Josephine simply ran into another corner.

"We're not getting anywhere," Mary Lou said shaking her head.

"Let's have another go at her." Kate bit the inside of her lip and thought for a moment. Then she walked as close as she dared. "Josephine, whose buried in that small grave, the one with the little white cross?"

"Ha, a little one, a very tiny one."

"A little what?"

She narrowed her eyes and wrinkled up her face. "Ha, wouldn't you like to know. Wouldn't everyone like to know?"

Kate gave an exasperated sigh. Josephine wasn't about to tell them anything. She probably doesn't know and is just making all this up. Then Kate had an idea.

"Josephine, do you like chocolate?"

"Love chocolate, Josephine loves chocolate." The woman rubbed her stomach in a circular motion and ran her tongue over her cracked lips.

"If I give you some chocolate, will you tell me?"

"Maybe." The old crone danced round and round then plopped herself into a wooden chair. She looked up at the girls; her beady eyes suddenly became expressive, even soft.

"I was young and pretty once, like you two. Yes I was. But I had to come here 'cause there was no place else for me to go. Had to come here." She looked off into the distance with a vacant stare. Then she covered her face with her hands and began to sob.

"Leave her alone, girls," the librarian said coming up to them. "Sometimes she gets this way when she remembers her past. Let her calm down. She'll be all right in a few minutes." The librarian led the girls away from the crumpled figure.

They went back to the stacks and continued their search for appropriate topics to write about.

Josephine looked after them, a look of sadness spreading across her face. Yes, sometimes her mind was clear and she remembered everything: her early life in the gutter, playing with the other urchins in the street, her parents always looking for work. When she was old enough she remembered helping her mother wash clothes. She watched the little ones born each year and die. One day her father didn't come home. No one could find him; no one cared.

Josephine remembered her budding body, her long blond hair, the way men noticed her. They touched her and offered her money. It felt good. So Josephine didn't wash clothes anymore.

She grimaced as she remembered the hands grabbing, pushing, and hurting her, their foul breath in her face. Then the cholera came. One by one the little ones died, then her mother died, too, and Josephine was alone. She went with the men; they gave her money; but sometimes she felt sick. She had a sore that wouldn't heal. After it went away there was a rash, fevers, sweats. She was afraid. Maybe she would die, too, like the others. The doctor said she had syphilis from sleeping with too many men. She would have to stop.

But how would she live? The doctor gave her injections. Oh how they hurt. Then they sent her here, to Hillside, where she had a warm bed and three meals a day. But people here were crazy. She would act crazy, too, so she could stay. What else could she do? She knew she would die in this place.

Josephine shook her head. Now everything was all jumbled up again. She sat in a corner and curled her sparse body into a ball and began rocking back and forth, moaning softly.

Chapter 10

As the next few weeks passed Mary Lou seemed to be coping better. She marked off each day on the calendar and vowed to put everything in perspective. These months would pass just like all the previous ones did. She remembered her experience in the Emergency Room: the stabbings, the shootings, the life and death struggles. She remembered feeling so helpless at the time, but it had passed and she had learned from it. She promised herself to learn from this experience, too.

Just before Christmas she and Kate were assigned to the Crib Room.

"I'm not looking forward to this," Mary Lou said as they trudged through the snow to the designated building.

"Yeah," Kate agreed. "Blanche said it was pretty disgusting." She blew out a breath as they opened the door and walked inside. A sickening stench hit them like a fist. It was a combination of urine, feces, and decaying flesh. Lysol combining with the other odors only made it worse. Their stomachs tightened in knots.

"You'll get used to it," Miss Dillard said looking at the expressions on the girls' faces. "You will spend two weeks on this ward. We're very short-handed and need the help."

Mary Lou swallowed hard to keep her breakfast down. Before them stood rows of adult-sized metal cribs, their white paint peeling in places revealing the rusty metal underneath. Dark stains ran down the sides. Each crib contained a living body. Some were terribly malformed, anomalies that should have died at birth, but, for some reason, didn't. Mary Lou was so surprised to see one patient with a huge head—a hydrocephalic who, against all odds, had lived to adulthood. Not really lived but survived to spend her last days staring at the ceiling, unable to turn her huge head. Some patients were kneeling, gripping the bars, chanting and moaning, or calling for loved ones who had abandoned them long ago.

A terrible sadness gripped Mary Lou. What crime had these wretches committed that they must pay such a terrible penalty?

She felt as though she had walked into one of Dante's levels of hell as she looked at those rows of once white metal cribs, not holding small cuddly infants, but, instead, smelly cursing adults.

"Mary, Mary, come here, my Mary." A scrawny hand reached out between the bars and grabbed Kate's scarf.

"Be careful," Miss Dillard cautioned. "Some of them scratch and bite."

"What type of treatment are these people given?" one student asked.

"Treatment?" Martha Dillard huffed, shook her head and uttered a dull hopeless sound. "Four teams work this ward. You can see them moving around. Two teams change the linen and diapers and the others treat the bedsores. At mealtime everyone feeds. At change of shift the next group continues where the previous ones left off."

She gave a deep sigh and shook her head. "It's not very rewarding work. That's why we're so short-staffed. We rotate people in and out of here. Otherwise they would quit. So we rely on the students for help. Does that answer your question?"

The girl grimaced, nodded and turned away.

A church group had come out to decorate the wards for Christmas. The artificial tree with its colored paper garlands reminded Mary Lou of grammar school: the garlands hanging askew, the tree perched at a precarious angle. It looked poignant and sad. That afternoon another group was scheduled to come in and sing Christmas carols.

Mary Lou and Kate were assigned to change linens. They grunted and tried to hide their disgust at the task. After all they had changed plenty of soiled linens during their three years of training, but this was a different world.

When the lunch trays arrived, they stopped, leaving the linen cart at the beginning of the next row of cribs so they could resume after feeding. Mary Lou watched the clock counting the hours until she could be free of this nightmarish place.

One woman lay in a catatonic state: her body rigid, her arms straight at her sides, eyes shut tight, lips pursed.

"Come on, Abby. It's time for lunch," an attendant said. She lowered the side of the crib and left the tray within reach. In a matter of moments the woman sat up, looked around to make sure no one was watching, and ate everything as fast as she could. Then she resumed her rigid position.

Mary Lou stared. "Does she do that all the time?"

"Been doing it for years," the attendant said. "Nobody knows why. Only comes alive to eat. Probably do it for the rest of her life. Doctors don't bother with these in here. Too far gone. Most just waitin' to die."

Kate carried a tray to another crib. An attendant called out a warning—too late. As Kate let down the side rail, the occupant lunged at her, spilling food and drink. Fingernails dug savagely into Kate's arm. A snarling sound issued from the woman's throat. Two attendants quickly jumped into action, roughly grabbing the woman's arms and legs. Both the patient and the attendants shouted obscenities at each other.

"No lunch for you today, Missy. You can just sit there in piss and rotting food, for all I care," one attendant hissed.

"Are you all right, Kate?" Mary Lou asked rushing over to her friend.

"I guess so, just a few scratches on my arm. What happened? What did I do wrong?"

"I tried to warn you, but it was too late," an attendant said. "Missy was gang raped when she was young. She lost all contact with reality and eventually ended up here. Been here for years. She's afraid of anybody she don't know. Usually Miss Dillard tells the students not to go near her. 'Her Highness' must of forgot this time." The woman raised her eyebrows and pursed her lips.

Missy sat in her crib glowering. Then she began to scrape the gooey mess of macaroni and cheese from her urine-soaked bed and shove it into her mouth.

Mary Lou hugged Kate. "This is just too awful," she said, tears filling her eyes.

At that point Miss Dillard appeared, her face set in a mask of displeasure. She examined Kate's arm, looked daggers at the attendants, and took Kate to the infirmary.

Mary Lou felt desolate without her friend. She stood staring at the room with its rows of fractured humanity. The tree and the meager decorations heralded the most joyous season of the year, but there was no joy here, only hopelessness and despair.

After lunch, which Mary Lou hardly touched, the girls went back to their task of changing beds. Kate seemed her usual cheery self, the angry red scratches on her arm covered with bright red merthiolate.

"See?" she said holding up her arm. "I match the season. Maybe I should paint the other arm green."

Mary Lou shook her head. "How I envy you. You seem to take everything in stride."

Kate shrugged. "Have to, Lulu. That's the only way to survive this place."

Later that afternoon the church group arrived. Two strong men set up a portable organ in a corner of the room. Three women joined the group. They all wore Santa Claus hats and dressed in red and green. Their smiling faces lent a somewhat festive air to the room. One robust woman sat down at the instrument and began to play. The familiar carols rang through the ward accompanied by strong voices, some a little off key, but no one paid attention.

A thin wail rose from one of the cribs. It was Missy. In her own way she was joining in. Then others began to sing.

"O Little Town of Bethlehem...." The familiar words and melodies sparked a chord in the recesses of some of their minds. Tears streamed down many an old creased face.

The students and attendants sang along. Even Abby came out of her catatonic state for a few moments. Missy reached her claw-like hand through the bars.

"Mary," she called. Mary, forgive me." Tears washed down her face running from her nose into her mouth. "Mary."

Kate went to her and carefully took her hand. "It's okay, Missy. I forgive you." She stood there holding the withered hand and patted it as they sang on.

After the grueling day in the Crib Room, Mary Lou and Kate trudged back to the nurses' home, their heads down, and their spirits low.

"I can't wait to get out of this uniform," Kate said. "It stinks of that place."

"Yeah," Mary Lou agreed.

They had just finished changing when someone knocked at their door. "Open up," Blanche said.

Mary Lou opened the door to her friend's beaming face.

"Carol's got a Christmas tree all set up in our room, just a little one, but it's a real one. Come on, we're going to have a lighting ceremony." She giggled. "We've even got fruit punch."

"But I thought we weren't supposed to have live trees, only artificial ones," Mary Lou said.

Blanche looked around as if expecting to see some authority figure, then whispered, "We sneaked it past old Dobins yesterday. Come on."

The girls ran after her to see all the others converged in Blanche and Carol's room. A two-foot tall tree sat on the desk, lights strung around, colored streamers hanging from the branches. Underneath, the girls had put cotton batting to look like snow.

"Now," Carol said theatrically, "every- body take some punch and we'll plug in the lights."

The laughing group reached for a paper cup of the fruit punch and held their breaths, as Carol was about to plug in the cord. A blood-curdling howl rent the air. The girls stood still, unable to move, their eyes wide with fear.

"What was that?" Mary Lou said as another howl followed, closer this time.

Carol ran to the window. "I don't see anything out there. Probably just an animal." She rubbed the goose bumps on her arms as she turned back. "Come on everyone, the tree."

As she plugged in the lights, a flash of electricity streaked along the defective cord. A bright spark fell on the cotton. The tree blazed up like a rocket. They stood, open-mouthed, unable to move as the flames danced and crackled through the dry branches.

"Quick, somebody get water," one of the girls shouted.

"Pull the plug out of the socket," someone yelled.

Kate grabbed a wastebasket, dumped the contents on the floor, and ran down the hall to the bathroom. She came back in a minute with the basket, dripping a trail of water behind her. With trembling hands Kate aimed the heavy basket at the burning tree and threw it. The stream of water missed its mark and spattered on the wall. The girls all stared, mesmerized.

As quickly as it started, the fire burned itself out leaving a smoldering mess. The girls looked at the charred remains, smoke rising from the ruin, and water dripping all around.

"Oh my gosh, what do we do now?" Mary Lou said.

"Open the window," Carol shouted between coughs. "The room's full of smoke."

Blanche opened the window ushering in the frigid air.

"What are we going to do with this tree?" Carol moaned.

"Throw it down the dust chute before old Dobins comes up here," Kate said.

Blanche and Carol picked up the remnants of the tree, wrapped it in an old sheet, poured more water, and stomped on it to make sure there was nothing smoldering inside. Then they sprinted down the hall to the utility room. The other girls cleaned up the water spills as best they could.

Within minutes all traces of the conflagration had disappeared. Only the acrid smell of smoke remained. The girls fled to their own rooms and locked their doors.

"What's burning up there?" Mrs. Dobins shrill voice called from the foot of the stairs. "Does somebody have a hot plate? If I find one, you'll all be in trouble."

The girls knew she wouldn't climb the stairs if she didn't have to. But the carefree moment had passed. Mary Lou couldn't get the sound of the mournful howling out of her head. Did it mean something ominous or was it just an animal?

Chapter 11

"Lulu, what are you doing? You didn't forget the Christmas carol service at the chapel, did you? Come on. Stop moping. You're not still thinking about that ghost, are you? There's nothing else to do here but study, and we've sure done enough of that." Kate looked at her roommate with a critical stare.

"I guess so. Maybe it'll get me out of this mood, but I can still hear that howling in my head. I'm kind of depressed tonight."

"You're depressed all the time," Kate said frowning. "Lighten up. We'll be out of here soon."

Mary Lou hesitated. "I didn't tell you, but I had another strange dream last night."

"What about?"

"About that same woman in the old Victorian house. It was like she was trying to tell me something." Mary Lou bit her lower lip and wrinkled her brow.

"It's just a dream. Forget about it. Come on, let's go to the service."

Mary Lou sighed and decided to follow Kate's advice. After all, it was only a dream, wasn't it? She didn't tell her friend that it was more vivid than the last one; that she felt as if she was actually there in that Victorian world. She tried to put it out of her mind.

The girls bundled up and went out into the frigid night. Stars twinkled in the clear winter sky. Snow crunched under their feet. The hairs in their noses stiffened with each breath. Blanche, Carol and Kate walked up ahead, giggling over some foolish joke.

Why don't they grow up? Mary Lou thought. They're so silly. No, let them laugh and enjoy themselves; I'm the one who's too serious. I'm the one who needs to laugh. She hurried up to reach her friends. "Wait up, what's so funny?"

"Oh," Carol said, doubling up with laughter. "You should have seen our waitress, Sally, this afternoon. She was so disturbed she was cursing up a storm, some of the foulest language I've ever heard. At first I thought she was mad at me, but then she whispered in my ear, 'Not you, honey, I'm talking to *him*.' She went on and on scolding this non-existent person. Finally Mrs. Morgan dragged her away and said she was relieved of her duties for the day. Some of the things she said." Carol shook her head and roller her eyes.

"Tell us, tell us," Blanche said.

"Never in a million years." With that she ran on ahead into the dark night.

The chapel, warm and snug, smelled of pine boughs and incense. A small crèche stood in one corner. It was a welcoming sight. Patients, attendants, staff, and a few visitors filled most of the pews.

The girls slid into the back.

"Look," Kate whispered, "there's Miss Dill Pickle."

"Where?" Mary Lou asked looking around.

"Over there, with those two male patients. One of them is the man she called Ben." Kate rolled her eyes. "See? She's holding his hand."

Miss Terry, the charge nurse of Cottage Ward number five sang at all social functions. Her rich soprano voice would have carried well in a concert hall, but most of those in the audience didn't realize how professional she sounded.

Josephine, wearing an old worn red dress, her hair combed and tied with a green bow, sat at the organ. She was a natural musician. Without a lesson in her life, she had learned to play the piano and the organ. One of the staff had tried to teach her to read music, but most of the time she improvised naturally. She sat, her head held high, her hands poised over the keys, waiting for a signal from Miss Terry.

The visiting minister led the congregation in traditional prayers, gave a short sermon about the joy of giving, and then turned the program over to Miss Terry.

She stood in the front of the chapel, her full breasts straining against her dark green velvet dress. A sprig of holly adorned her red hair.

She nodded to Josephine and prepared to sing. Josephine, in a world of her own, paid no attention. Miss Terry sighed and whispered, "We're ready to begin. Play "Silent Night", please."

Josephine lifted her head, as if suddenly aware of where she was, and began to play. The familiar strains of "Silent Night" and "O Little Town of Bethlehem" filled the chapel. Miss Terry's rich voice rose above the organ.

Suddenly Josephine stopped playing. Miss Terry stopped singing. Everyone waited while Josephine looked around as if wondering where she was. Then she seemed to blank out for a moment. When she began to play again, it wasn't a carol that issued from the instrument, but "Good Night Irene".

Miss Terry was disconcerted. She didn't know quite what to do. Then she shrugged her shoulders and began to sing: "Good night Irene, I'll see you in my dreams...."

The congregation laughed. Some patients stamped their feet. They all joined in the singing, managed to finish the service with "O Come All Ye Faithful".

During the night Mary Lou woke to another spine-chilling howl. She pulled the covers up over her head, but the sound continued. *What is it?*

She slid out of bed, glanced at her sleeping roommate, and crept to the window.

The full moon lit up the desolate landscape. In the distance Mary Lou saw movement. It could be the animal they saw at the cemetery. But something else was out there, too. A white floating object seemed to be following the animal as it ran behind a building.

Mary Lou cringed, shut her eyes, and shook her head. When she looked out again, everything was still and calm. Had she imagined the whole thing or was there really a ghost roaming around Hillside?

Chapter 12

Mary Lou and Kate had been working on the open wards for the two weeks before the scheduled Christmas break. They talked with the patients, played cards and checkers, and walked up and down the wards with those that needed assistance. During this time they wore their school uniforms and caps. This attire seemed to impress most of the patients. They treated the girls with respect realizing that the white uniforms and caps designated them as authority figures.

Some of the patients seemed so normal that sometimes Mary Lou almost forgot where she was. Then an argument would break out—attendants running in separating two screaming women pulling each other's hair. No, nothing was normal here. She was in a mad-house. Her stomach tightened; her breathing quickened, until she regained control. That night she scratched off another day from the calendar.

"Have you decided which patient you're going to use for your case study?" Kate asked looking up from her book.

"Uh huh. Have you?" Mary Lou said.

Kate screwed up her face. "Maybe. Remember that patient on the post-lobotomy ward that Dill Pickle was talking to—so chummy like?"

"Yeah, Ben, the one she was with at the chapel the other night."

Kate nodded. "I think I'll check his chart. He might have an interesting history. We have some free time now," she said. "What do you say we go check out this *Ben?*"

"Okay." Mary Lou shrugged. She, too, was curious about Miss Dillard's interest in this particular patient. Maybe some research would help her focus on the real world.

They bundled up and walked to the building that housed the post-lobotomy ward. Most of the patients sat in hard-backed chairs, staring at the floor or looking into space. There was no need for restraints on this ward. The patients lived in a world detached from reality.

The girls told the charge nurse why they were there and she granted permission for them to review the charts. Kate thumbed through a number of paper folders stacked on a rack. Mary Lou looked through another. Since they didn't know the last name, they had to look at every male patient's first name.

"I think I found it," Kate whispered excitedly. "Ben Turner, MD. MD? Well what do you know about that? He's a doctor." She looked at Mary Lou, her eyes wide and her mouth agape.

"Come on. Let's sit here at the nurses' station and take notes." She turned to the admission and history sheet and began to write. "Admitted, September 14, 1935. Diagnosis, acute Schizophrenia. No response to Electroconvulsive Therapy or Insulin Coma Therapy. Combative and uncooperative. Pre-frontal lobotomy performed on January 12, 1938. Wow."

Suddenly a shadow fell across the chart. The girls looked up to see Miss Dillard standing above them frowning, her arms crossed over her chest. "What are you two doing here?" she demanded.

"We're looking at charts, for our case studies," Kate stammered.

The instructor looked down and grabbed the chart from Kate's hand. "Not that one." She took a deep breath. Then slowly let it out. Her expression changed from one of anger to one of authority. "You can find much more interesting cases on Ward C." The look she gave them said, "hands off".

"Yes Ma'am."

They picked up their things and hurried away. Kate stuffed the notes she had managed to scribble into her pocket. When they reached the doorway, Mary Lou looked back and saw Miss Dillard talking to the charge nurse and shaking her finger.

As they walked quickly into the hallway, they saw a young doctor walking toward them. He smiled.

"Oh my God," Kate whispered. "Isn't he the one who was asking Dr. Forester all those questions?"

Before Mary Lou could answer, he walked up to them. "Good afternoon, Ladies. What are you two doing here? You have guilty looks on your faces." He raised his eyebrows and smiled.

"Uh,...." Kate stammered. "We were just looking at charts for a patient to use for our case studies."

He nodded. "Most of the post-lobotomy patients have pretty interesting histories. Did you find one?" When he looked at Mary Lou, his blue eyes softened.

She felt uneasy, took a deep breath, and then looked back. "Miss Dillard told us to go to another ward. She seemed angry when we looked at a particular chart." She half expected him to provide them with an answer.

He shook his head. "She's a strange one. I've been here for a year now and haven't been able to figure her out. Try Ward C. Most of those patients have interesting backgrounds. See you around." He walked away whistling to himself.

Kate and Mary Lou exchanged glances and left the building.

"He sure is good looking," Kate said.

"And nice, too," Mary Lou added.

When they were back in their room, Kate said, "I have a feeling there's some history between Dill Pickle and Doctor Ben Turner."

Mary Lou shrugged. "So now you're a detective, huh? She does seem to be overly protective of him. I wonder why."

"I'll bet Josephine knows," Kate said. "She seems to know everything around here. Maybe we should buy her lots of chocolate and grill her." She gave Mary Lou a conspiratorial wink.

"We'll see. Or, maybe we should mind our own business."

"Oh that wouldn't be any fun. After the Christmas break we'll see what we can find out," Kate said. "Can't let this go of this juicy tidbit."

Chapter 13

Mary Lou watched Kate pack her suitcase: shirts, sweaters, and two pairs of shoes. "Will you need all that for one week?" she asked. "Sure," Kate said. "We're going to my grandmother's house in Kenosha. That's in Wisconsin, just in case you didn't know." She gave Mary Lou a sly look and a wink. "We always cut down our own Christmas tree out in the woods. It's a lot of fun. Last year my uncle cut such a spindly one that we had to fill it with extra strings of popcorn and cranberries." She began to laugh as she crammed more clothes in the case.

Mary Lou sighed. I wish I were going with her, she thought. She sat on the bed sorting through the few items she planned to take with her to her home in Rockford.

"So, what's your family doing this Christmas?" Kate asked as she opened yet another drawer.

"The same every year. Nothing very exciting," Mary Lou answered. "My Aunt Phyllis and her two dull daughters come over. We go to church, eat dinner, then open gifts. Same thing every year—no surprises. Honest, I'd love it if somebody came over dressed like Santa Claus, just once, and burst in with a pack on his back, laughing and saying, 'ho, ho, ho.' That's what they do at Bill's house."

"Isn't there anybody who could do that?" Kate asked.

"No. My mother would probably have a hissy fit. I can hear her. 'Christmas is a religious holiday. We shouldn't be celebrating pagan customs'."

"What's pagan about Old St. Nick?" Kate asked.

"I haven't a clue. Who knows what goes on in her head? The only part of the week I'm looking forward to is the last day. Bill is coming to pick me up and we'll exchange gifts then." Mary Lou smiled, anticipating spending the whole day with Bill.

"That's a nifty wallet you bought him," Kate said. "I wonder what he got for you?"

Mary Lou shrugged. "You know, Bill and I have both been so busy lately that sometimes I worry that we might be drifting apart."

"Oh no, Lulu. He's a great guy. You mustn't think that. As soon as we get out of here, everything will go back to normal."

"No it won't," Mary Lou said. "Nothing will ever be the same again."

Mary Lou climbed onto a bus to downtown Chicago. There she boarded a Greyhound bus for home to her mother, her aunt and her two cousins. She had nothing in common with any of them.

When Mary Lou walked into the house, her mother gave her a critical look. "You're pale and there are dark circles under your eyes. Have you been getting enough sleep?"

"Yes, Mother, but I've been studying a lot. It's probably eye strain." She looked at the tree—a white artificial one with every ornament in place. I wonder if she measures them with a ruler, she thought. For a moment she remembered the incident with Carol's Christmas tree and smiled. There was little to smile about here. It was the same thing every year. She could count on that.

Mary Lou vaguely remembered a time when there was laughter in that house, but it was so long ago. She, a young child, riding on Daddy's shoulders, squealing in delight as he galloped around the Christmas tree, laughing and singing.

Mother screaming, "You'll drop her!" and grabbing her away. The child cried, reaching for her father. She tried to keep that memory alive, but as the years passed, it receded farther and farther away.

After dinner, to make conversation, Mary Lou described some of her experiences at Hillside, without embellishment.

"Don't talk about such things, dear. They're too depressing," her mother said shaking her head and wringing her hands. So she sat in silence waiting for the hours to pass.

Mary Lou could imagine the fun at Bill's house: the girls all dressed up, excitedly oohing and ahhing over each gift. Bill's mother had invited her to stay with them, but Mary Lou felt an obligation to go home. Her mother was a lonely woman: depressive, negative, with few friends.

If only Mary Lou had grown up with her father instead of her mother. What wonderful times they would have had. She imagined herself living with him in Germany: Fraulein Hammond.

"Mary Louise, stop daydreaming. Come and say goodbye to Aunt Phyllis and your cousins. They're leaving. Be a good girl."

"Yes Mother." Good girl, good girl, always be a good girl. Someday I'd like to be a bad girl, she thought, just to see what it feels like.

Mary Lou wondered why Bill hadn't called yet. It was getting late. She kept looking at the clock and then at the telephone willing it to ring. She almost jumped out of her chair when it finally did, at almost nine o'clock.

Her mother answered it then, with a frown, handed it to her. "It's for you. That young man."

Why does she always refer to him as 'that young man'? It irritated Mary Lou. She took the phone and said softly, "Hello."

"Merry Christmas, Honey," Bill said.

"And to you, too," she answered. "Are you all having a good time at your house?"

He hesitated for a moment. "There's a problem. My mom just got a call. My grandfather had a heart attack, so we're leaving for Milwaukee in a few minutes."

"Oh," was all she could say.

"Mary Lou, I'm sorry, but I won't be able to pick you up on Saturday like we planned. I don't know when we'll be back. It all depends on grandpa's condition."

She hesitated, swallowed hard and tried to control her emotions. "That's okay. I understand. I can take the bus." She fought back the tears that welled up in her eyes.

"We'll see each other when you get back to Hillside, okay?" he asked.

"Sure. See you then."

When she hung up the phone, Mary Lou quickly wiped away the tears that managed to sneak out. Her mother stood there, her arms folded across her chest.

"Bill won't be able to pick me up. His grandfather had a heart attack," she explained.

"Humph. Men, they always disappoint you. You'd better learn that lesson now, Mary Louise."

"I'm tired," Mary Lou said. "I think I'll go to bed. Good night Mother."

She tossed and turned lying awake for a long time. When she finally fell into a fitful sleep, she dreamed of Bill. He was walking away from her. She called to him. He looked back once, and then kept walking. Then Margaret Montague stood be-fore her reaching out her arms as if imploring Mary Lou for help.

She woke with a start just as the rising sun peaked through the Venetian blinds. Shuddering, she quickly dressed and went down to breakfast.

On the bus ride back, she tried to remember the dream but it was all jumbled in her mind. She dismissed it as a result of Bill's disappointing phone call.

Mary Lou was almost glad to get back to Hillside. At least there she was with friends. They talked, they laughed, they cried. They were alive. That was it. Her mother wasn't living. She merely existed like so many of the inmates here. Mary Lou promised herself she wouldn't be like her mother. She would live each day to its fullest.

Chapter 14

The following week Bill met Mary Lou at the nearby restaurant. When Mary Lou came back, Kate looked at her eagerly. "You weren't gone very long."

"No, he was in a hurry to get back. Said he had a lot of work to do." She threw her coat and hat on a chair and plopped on the bed.

"How did he like the wallet you gave him?" Kate asked.

"Okay, I guess. He said it was nice."

"Aren't you going to tell me what he gave you?" Kate persisted.

Mary Lou reached into her purse and took out a small box. She opened it to reveal a pair of silver earrings.

"Ooh," Kate said, "earrings to match your silver chain."

"Uh huh."

Kate picked one up. "These are for pierced ears." She looked at Mary Lou, a question on her face.

"I don't think he ever wondered whether my ears are pierced or not." Her lower lip trembled.

"Are you going to get them pierced?"

"That's not the point, is it? He never asked, never noticed. Does he even care?" She put them back in the box and shoved it in a drawer.

The next assignment took the students to 13, the women's violent ward. It was a nightmare world. The smells were more of the same: all mixing with the odor of madness and despair. It could only be described as decay of the spirit. It was worse than the Crib Room. These patients were mobile except for a few who were restrained.

One old woman, bent like a question mark, greeted the students at the door, nodding her head, mumbling obscenities, her fetid breath reaching out with each cackle. She held a tin drinking cup in her hand waving it around and wrinkling her face at the students. Gingerly she pushed it toward Kate. Soft odorous feces filled the cup to the brim.

Kate turned her face away in disgust. The woman danced around laughing, a sound that wasn't quite human.

"Matilda," Miss Dillard scolded. "Go along. No one appreciates your sick humor." She looked around for an attendant. "Take this woman away," she ordered.

The attendant grabbed the old woman and pulled her along as she caressed the cup to her bosom, crooning to it as if it were a living thing.

Miss Dillard shook her head then turned to the students and indicated a long room lined with tall windows. Worn linoleum covered the floor. Its pattern long ago obscured by hundreds of shuffling feet. "This is the day room where patients spend most of their time."

Emaciated disheveled looking hags walked round and round aimlessly, some weeping, some staring into space. Mary Lou wrapped her arms around herself as she felt the drafts seeping in around the old warped window frames.

All the women wore simple cotton shifts, a washed-out blue-gray. Some wore sweaters. Others rubbed their arms in an effort to keep warm. But one woman stood out from the others. She wore nothing at all, walking around and mumbling in a foreign tongue. Her skin was tinged with blue from the cold, but she seemed oblivious to the chill. Methodically, she pulled on one breast and then the other, chanting the same incomprehensible words over and over. Her breasts hung down to her navel, the skin so stretched it looked like parchment. They slapped against her sagging abdomen as she walked.

"That's Rose," Miss Dillard said in response to their startled looks. "The staff has tried everything to keep her clothed. She gets out of the most complex knots. One assistant even tried sewing her clothes on. Within an hour she was naked again. No one knows what goes on in her tortured mind. She keeps that up until she drops from exhaustion at night only to begin again the next morning."

On their first day they witnessed the torment some of these people lived with. One woman walked through the ward with her hands over her ears, a frantic look on her face.

"Make them stop! Please make them stop! The voices—they're so loud—saying terrible things—I can't stand it." She walked round and round, wide-eyed, as if looking for a place to hide, but there was nowhere for her to go. No wonder these poor souls looked eagerly for the paraldehyde, Mary Lou thought. That was the only sedative available to them. At least the vile stuff put them in a semi-stuporous state for a little while. Then everything would start all over again.

Miss Dillard led them into an adjoining room. "This is the tub room."

Huge bathtubs lined the walls, each occupied by a patient. Canvas tops secured around the rim kept them from climbing out. Only an opening for the head allowed for feeding.

"Warm water flows continuously in and out of the tub calming the disturbed ones," Miss Dillard said.

Mary Lou's eyes widened as she looked at the disembodied heads lolling against the canvas: some slept; some sang songs; others shouted and cursed. "How long do they stay in there?"

The instructor shrugged. "A few hours, some all day. The attendants feed them at mealtimes and clean out the tubs at the end of the shift."

Mary Lou cringed at the thought of those tubs full of excrement. I'm glad I don't have to do that, she thought.

Mary Lou followed Miss Dillard to the medicine room, her assignment for the morning.

The instructor opened the locked door. "The only medication you will dispense is paraldehyde. Each patient receives three-quarters of an ounce."

Mary Lou took the large blue bottle off the shelf and checked the name of the drug on the label. She tried desperately to control her shaking hands. When she removed the stopper fumes of the strong liquid escaped. She pulled back for a moment, surprised by the pungent odor.

"Don't inhale too much of that," Miss Dillard warned.

Mary Lou nodded and proceeded to carefully prepare the thick medicine glasses, filling each one with the exact amount. Miss Dillard watched her with an eagle eye. Two burly attendants stood beside her. The tray trembled in her grip as picked it up and looked toward the day room. I have to go out there, she thought, sensing a trembling in her knees. The attendants looked at her; Miss Dillard gave her an encouraging nod, and she walked into the day room.

"Now don't let them intimidate you, Hammond," the instructor said following behind her. "They'll all want their medication at the same time. The attendants will keep them in line. Just hand each patient a medicine glass, watch her drink it, and take the glass back. Be sure none of them pockets one. A broken glass makes an effective weapon. Don't be afraid. They can smell fear." Miss Dillard's eyes narrowed as she stared at Mary Lou.

I wonder if terror smells the same as fear, Mary Lou thought. Her hands felt icy cold gripping the metal tray.

"Everybody line up," an attendant shouted. They flanked Mary Lou, one on each side, as the patients crowded around. No one formed any kind of a line. Mary Lou knew her knees would buckle at any minute. With sheer willpower, she stiffened her legs and began handing out the medicines, watching as the patients gulped down the burning liquid. It must be like a shot of liquor, she thought.

She was almost finished, just a few more, when a face loomed in front of her: vacuous eyes, lank greasy hair, and oily pimpled skin.

"Mary...had...a...little...lamb...little lamb...little lamb...."

The face went blank for a moment. Mary Lou recognized the petit mal seizure that Miss Dillard had described, the temporary loss of contact with reality in some epileptics. Her trembling hand held out the glass of paraldehyde. As the woman came out of her trance-like state, her eyes flared with fury. In a flash she knocked the glass out of the girl's hand and pounced. Mary Lou fell to the floor under the sudden impact; medicine glasses rolled on the linoleum spilling their oily contents. The woman screamed; others screamed. The attendants tore into the patient, but her strong hands circled Mary Lou's throat in a vise-like grip.

Miss Dillard dove into the melee. Mary Lou's last recollection before the darkness closed in was the fetid breath blowing in her face and the words, "Mary had a little lamb...."

"Hammond! Hammond, are you all right?"

She could hear someone calling her from a distance. Who was it? Slowly she opened her eyes, as Miss Dillard's anxious face came into focus.

"Are you all right?" The woman sounded genuinely concerned.

"I think so," she whispered rubbing her neck. "It happened so fast."

"Those damned attendants! They're supposed to protect the students. Administration will hear about this."

Miss Dillard bundled Mary Lou in her coat and hat. "We'll get you back to the nurses' residence where you'll rest for the remainder of the day."

"Please don't leave me alone. I'm so afraid."

"There's no need to be frightened," Miss Dillard said. "We try to protect the students from bodily harm. This was an incident that never should have happened. The attendants were not doing their jobs."

What am I afraid of? Mary Lou asked herself. The patients can't hurt me in my room. It's something else, something I can't see; I can only feel it and hear it in the night.

Miss Dillard looked down at Mary Lou. For a moment a look of tenderness crossed her face, but she quickly replaced it with her mask of professionalism. "I'll have your roommate excused also. She can sit with you. I'll have a liquid tray sent up to you for supper. Later Dr. Corbett will come by and examine you."

Mary Lou heard the sounds of the ward all jumbled up in the distance as she slowly walked away, Miss Dillard supporting her. As they left Josephine came dancing by, turning round and round.

"I know a secret. I know a secret," she repeated in her singsong fashion. "Flowers in the cemetery. I know a secret."

Miss Dillard turned to her, a stern look of anger on her face. "You know nothing, do you hear me? Nothing. Stop making up stories, Josephine, or I'll punish you."

The woman laughed her distinctive cackle and danced away.

Mary Lou sat staring out the window of her room, a scarf wrapped around her neck. The wind seeped in around the window frame. Its tendrils crept toward her, chilling her frightened body. She shivered and wrapped her robe tighter.

"Are you okay?" Kate asked anxiously. She looked up from her book at the frightened look on her friend's face.

"I guess so. It was so scary, but it was partly my fault. I let the woman get too close. I should have called one of the attendants."

"Baloney," Kate said. "Those attendants are supposed to be watching us while we pass out the booze. They're lazy and they don't give a damn."

Mary Lou thought for a while. "You know, Josephine came around after it happened while Miss Dillard was walking me back here. She said a very strange thing."

"She always talks nonsense. Nobody listens to her. Miss Flank says she makes everything up as an attention getting mechanism. She's not as loony as she seems."

"That's just the point. She danced around singing about knowing a secret, about flowers in the cemetery."

Kate's eyes widened as she scooted closer to her friend.

"Remember in the library when we asked her? She said she knew. Now she said it again, in front of Dillard."

"What did Dill Pickle say?"

"She was furious. She told Josephine to stop making up stories, that she knows nothing, that she'd punish her if she kept it up. What do you think of that?"

"Hmm, interesting. Maybe we ought to have another talk with Josephine."

"I was thinking the same thing," Mary Lou said in a hoarse voice. "The next time one of us gets her alone, we'll try again."

"You'd better stop talking now," Kate said. "You sound worse."

A little later Miss Dillard brought the doctor to examine Mary Lou. She was pleasantly surprised when she recognized the same handsome young doctor they had met on the Post-Lobotomy Ward.

"This is Dr. Corbett," Miss Dillard said. "And the student is Mary Lou Hammond." She nodded to the doctor.

"I believe Miss Hammond and I have already met." He looked down at her and smiled. He rubbed his hands together for a moment. "I don't want to examine you with cold hands," he said. Then he expertly probed the tissues around her neck and looked down her throat.

His hands are so gentle, Mary Lou thought. He isn't even hurting me.

"There is some swelling here," he said when he had finished, "but I don't think it's anything serious. You should be as good as new in the morning. Get a good night's sleep and stay on liquids for tonight. If you have any problems swallowing, let Miss Dillard know and I'll see you again."

She nodded her thanks as they left the room.

"Boy, he's a dream," Kate said. "Maybe I should accidentally get hurt, nothing serious of course. I wouldn't mind him examining me."

Mary Lou shook her head. Kate never took anything seriously. She was so lucky.

Mary Lou lay awake, staring at the ceiling. Her swollen throat made swallowing difficult. She decided to prop herself up and read for a while. The first book she grabbed was on the history of psychiatry. This will be on the exam next week, so I'd better review, she thought.

Let's see now, 'early civilization based their prognoses on such things as numbers, astrology, configuration of the entrails of animals,' yuck, that sounds disgusting. What else? 'Extrasensory perception and the interpretation of dreams.'

She looked out the window at the bleak landscape. Interpretation of dreams, hmm. Who could interpret them? She had read that dreams should not be taken literally, but her dreams were so specific, more like a moving picture than a disconnected dream. I'd better get a hold of myself before I go bananas. It won't be long until we leave this place and I can forget all about it.

Maybe I should tell Bill about the dreams. No, he'll think his girl friend is a nut case. Besides, he's so busy with school I don't want him worrying about me.

She picked up the book and read on. 'Water was one of the elements used for purification. It is still being used today in hydrotherapy. Power was attributed to the utterance of certain words—the healer and the medicine man repeated the same words over and over.' I guess they thought the spirits would get tired of hearing them and leave the poor guy alone. She smiled at the picture in her mind: medicine men wearing bizarre masks and headdresses dancing around the possessed individual and chanting.

'Drugs were prepared according to secret rituals. The healers used emetics, cathartics, blood-letting and trephining to get rid of evil spirits.' How in the world did they make holes in people's skulls without killing them? Imagine the number of infections. Oh well, some of them lived. Anthropologists had found skulls way back from the time of the early Egyptians with holes burred into them.

'Lycanthropy: the patient imagines him- self to be a wolf or other animal, lead to the werewolf legend.' That's interesting, just the kind of question Miss Dillard will ask. She underlined it in the book.

Plato, Aristotle, Middle Ages...can't read anymore...so tired. Her eyes grew heavy. Without realizing it, she picked up the pencil and began to scribble something on her notepad. As she yawned, the books and papers slipped to the floor. Despite the fact that Bill had the clasp on her silver chain repaired, it fell from her neck, landing on the notepad. It looked as though the clasp had been deliberately opened.

Mary Lou slept, but not a restful sleep. She thrashed about in bed and dreamed.

Two women...Margaret Montague...Agnes Calumet...silver tea service on the table...talking about an unfaithful husband...planning divorce...cutting of funds....

Chapter 15

Kate reached for the alarm clock, fumbling with the switch. She turned on the light beside her bed and, through sleepy eyes, saw Mary Lou sitting up staring into space.

"Hey Lulu, what goes on? You look like you're in a trance or something."

"Oh Kate," Mary Lou sobbed. "I think I'm losing my mind."

Kate hurried over to her friend sat on the bed, took her in her arms, and gave her a hug.

"I had another dream, just like the others. And look at the note on the floor." Mary Lou's body shook with fear.

"It's this place, Lulu. It's getting to you. Why just yesterday Sue was sure she was a schizophrenic. You'll be all right when we're out of here and back to the real world."

Kate reached down for the note. It was mirror-image writing. She couldn't make out anything.

"Hold it up to the mirror," Mary Lou said.

Kate slid off the bed. As she held the paper toward the mirror, the words jumped out at her.

That is how it happened to me.
I was strangled.
My body lies in the graveyard.
Margaret Montague

Kate felt a chill run up her spine. "This isn't your handwriting. Who is this Margaret Montague?" she asked, fear showing on her face.

"She's the lady in my dream, I'm sure of it. The one who lives in the Victorian mansion. I think I heard her name in the dream last night. I think her spirit is trying to tell me something. The writing is hers."

"Come on, you don't believe in ghosts, do you?" Kate looked at her roommate and bit the side of her lip.

"I don't know what I believe. I'm so scared."

Kate sat down on the bed again. The girls were quiet for a long time.

Then Kate nodded and her face brightened. "Okay, let's go about this whole thing systematically. We'll keep a log; write down the dreams as soon as you wake up. Your subconscious wrote a message before each dream. Maybe that means something. So, put everything down in chronological order. Then we'll see if there's any logic to the whole thing. I'll bet there won't be any more dreams or messages."

Mary Lou looked down at the floor, a dejected expression on her face. "You're wrong. There will be more. This woman feels real to me. She's trying to tell me something. I have to help her."

"How can you help someone who's been dead all this time?" Kate asked. "Do you hear how silly that sounds? Come on, let's get dressed or we'll be late. Oh, and here's your silver chain, on the floor. I thought Bill had it fixed for you."

"He did."

As Mary Lou walked toward 13, she met Miss Dillard.

"Hammond, I've been looking for you. Come into my office." She led the girl into a room, bare except for a desk, a chair and a bookcase. Martha Dillard was not one for frivolities. But Mary Lou did notice a single rose in a bud vase on the desk. That was definitely out of character. It lent a poignant touch to this very private person.

Mary Lou had the feeling that Miss Dillard was harboring a secret deep within her shapeless bosom.

"I want to be certain you are ready to return to duty. How do you feel?"

"Okay, I guess. My throat is a little sore and still feels swollen, but, otherwise I'm fine." She tried to sound convincing but her voice sounded flat, even to herself.

"You look like you haven't been sleeping well. You have dark circles around your eyes."

"I haven't," Mary Lou admitted. "I've been having strange dreams." She thought for a moment, and then decided to confide in Miss Dillard. "Something about a Victorian woman who was murdered here." As soon as she saw the expression on the face of her instructor, she knew it was a mistake.

"Dreams are common in a setting like this. Many of the students complain of nightmares. Some even imagine they see things. Some roaming around the old cemetery claim they see a ghost. I'd advise you to stay away from there. You're a very impressionable young lady and your mind can conjure up all sorts of images. Is that clear?" Miss Dillard's face took on a stern expression as if she knew of the girls' excursions to the cemetery.

"You've been out there, haven't you?" she asked in an accusing tone. "I can see it on your face. Stay away from there. It's not a pleasant place, just full of memories and pain." For a moment her face took on a far away look, then she snapped back.

"Now, if you feel up to it, go back to 13. I've left instructions that you are not to pass medicines. You will be accompanied by an attendant at all times, one I can trust."

"Yes Ma'am." Mary Lou stood to leave. For a moment Miss Dillard looked at her with an expression of tenderness. But it passed quickly as her face resumed its mask of efficiency. It seemed to say keep your distance.

The day passed without further incident. Mary Lou tried to remain as detached as possible. She assisted in feeding those who couldn't, or wouldn't, feed themselves. The attendants kept all the students away from Big Red, an enormous woman built like a wrestler. She spent her days either in the tub or chained to her bed. The story circulated that she had brutally killed an attendant years ago. Was it true? None of the girls was willing to find out. In the afternoon Mary Lou heard a woman screaming, the same woman she had seen the first day. "Make them stop, please make them stop! They're saying terrible things to me, dirty things."

"Can't anyone help that poor woman?" Mary Lou asked the charge nurse.

She shook her head. "Edna, give her an extra dose of paraldehyde," she called to an attendant. "The doctors have tried Electro-Convulsive Therapy, Insulin Shock Therapy and Metrazol Convulsive Therapy. No results. She's pitiful. She used to be an actress, starred in a lot of mystery thrillers and horror films. Pretty soon she began believing the stories were true and ended up here. The family won't permit a lobotomy; that would put an end to the terrors and the voices."

"But what will happen to her?" Mary Lou asked.

"She'll keep on hearing voices until they tell her to do something drastic. The last one we had drowned herself in one of the tubs. This one's not so bad. She doesn't hear the voices constantly, at least not yet, but someday...."

"Excuse me, please. Excuse me, please." A petite anxious looking woman came up to the charge nurse. "Mrs. Pearson, have you seen my baby? They haven't let me hold her yet? When can I see my baby?" She kept wringing her hands.

Mrs. Pearson took the woman's arms firmly in her hands. "Sally, you know you don't have a baby. Now go away and stop bothering me."

"I do so have a baby. I do so have a baby," she repeated over and over.

"Look," the nurse said, "there's Priscilla waiting for you. Why don't you go over and tell her a story?"

"Yes Ma'am," Sally said. She walked away, head bowed, arms cradling a non-existed infant.

Mary Lou looked quizzically at the charge nurse.

Miss Pearson let out a sigh and shook her head. "That poor woman had a post-partum psychosis. Some depression is common after birth in many women, but it usually doesn't last long. The more serious cases have to be hospitalized for a while, but usually return home. Sally's was a particularly severe case. She thought her baby was evil, the child of Satan. She killed the poor little thing, but doesn't remember any of it. Her husband was devastated. He left her here, took his two daughters and moved away.

"Sally has been asking for her baby for the last ten years. She'll probably continue for the rest of her life." Mrs. Pearson looked at her watch. "It's time for class. Miss Dillard gave me specific instructions to see that the students are on time. Go along now. I'll see you tomorrow. And, Miss Hammond, get some rest. You look pale and tired."

"I will, Mrs. Pearson, and thank you."

Maybe I'll do my case study on that woman, Mary Lou thought. But she was too tired to think anymore about it now.

After class, seeing Miss Dillard in the hall, Mary Lou stopped to discuss an assignment. Then she went back to her room.

"Hi Lulu, what kept you?" Kate asked. "I saw you talking to Dill Pickle."

"I was just asking her about that paper we're supposed to write. I think I'll do it on developmental disorders. She said it was okay."

"Why developmental disorders? Everybody else chose psychoses or neuroses."

"I know," Mary Lou said plopping into a chair. "But I want to see if I can find some reason for this mirror-image writing of mine. Maybe if I can understand it, I'll feel better. Maybe I can find out why

I'm having these dreams, getting these messages. I told Miss Dillard about the dreams. She said it's not uncommon and not to worry about it."

"See? Even old Dill Pickle can give some good advice once in a while." Kate smiled.

"Oh Kate, I wish I had never come to this terrible place." She threw herself on the bed and buried her face in the pillow.

Kate sat next to her. "There's nothing wrong with you. You've been writing backwards since you were a kid. Other people do that, too. I remember a boy at a Christmas party once. The windows were all frosty. He wrote on them backwards with his fingernail and we all had to run outside to read it. You're not so strange."

Kate's voice had a soothing quality about it. "Look you're all hunched over, like you're tied up in knots." She grabbed Mary Lou's shoulders and began kneading them with her fingers.

"Ow! that hurts."

"Sure it does. Your muscles are all knotted up. Just relax and let me loosen them."

Mary Lou laid her arms across the desk and put her head down. Within a few minutes she began to relax under Kate's expert ministrations. "Maybe you should become a masseuse," she said.

"Yeah, sure. Is that better now?"

"Much. Thanks. I am making a mountain out of a molehill. Now I'm sleepy, think I'll take a nap. Wake me in time for supper, will you?"

"Okay."

Kate closed the door quietly when she was sure that Mary Lou had fallen into a deep sleep. That's what she needs, she thought. I don't know what to do. I'm so worried. Maybe there's something really wrong with her. Should I talk to somebody about this? Maybe I should tell Bill or that cute Dr. Corbett. Now I'm the one who's making a mountain out of a molehill. This'll all pass once we get out of here.

Chapter 16

"Today a group of you will begin working in Hydrotherapy," Miss Dillard said. "I told you at the beginning of the rotation that you would experience some of the treatments before assisting with patients. Water therapy is scheduled for this morning. The following students please report to Hydro." She rattled off the names including Mary Lou and Kate. "The rest of you come with me."

"Thanks a lot, Dill Pickle," Kate muttered. "I'm not going to let anybody wrap me in those cold wet sheets. You know how claustrophobic I get." She looked at Mary Lou with real fear in her eyes.

"Don't worry. If you get too uncomfortable, I'll unwrap you right away," Mary Lou said squeezing her friend's hand.

"Promise?"

"Promise."

A tall grim-faced woman greeted them as they filed into the Hydro room. She introduced herself as Miss Porter. Her lank hair hung down around her sallow expressionless face. She could have been one of the patients. Three cots covered with rubber sheets sat side-by-side ready for the demonstration. An attendant placed a wet sheet over each cot.

"All right, Ladies. The first three of you strip down to your panties," the instructor said. She indicated Kate and two of her classmates.

Kate frowned as she and the other students began to undress. They were noticeably uncomfortable stripping in front of each other.

"Come on, girls," cajoled the instructor. "None of you has anything new. You've all seen it before."

Kate reluctantly climbed onto the narrow cot. "Lulu," she whispered, "wrap me loose so I don't have a panic attack."

"Okay, I'll try."

The girls began squealing as goose bumps rose on their skin from the cold sheets.

"I'm freezing," one of the girls shouted through chattering teeth.

"You'll warm up in a minute," Miss Porter said. "Here now, let me demonstrate." She pulled the loose sheet out of Mary Lou's hand. "You have to wrap it tighter. Pull the sheet over the right arm and tuck it under the left side of the body."

Kate took a deep breath as she felt the restraining sheet compress her chest. Her eyes widened in fear.

"Someone on the opposite side pulls the other side of the sheet over the left arm, like this, tucking it securely under the right side. Now, you have your patient adequately restrained."

Kate began to take rapid short breaths as she realized she couldn't move. She moaned and tried to squirm.

"Now cover her with a blanket and she should be warmed and relaxed in a few minutes," Miss Porter continued apparently oblivious to Kate's distress.

"Get me out of here," Kate gasped. "I can't breathe." Her face turned red as she began panting. "Just relax, dear. Don't fight it. You'll be fine." Miss Porter patted Kate's head as she thrashed it from side to side.

"Let me out!" Kate screamed. "I can't stand it!"

"She's claustrophobic," Mary Lou said. "We've got to unwrap her before she passes out." Her trembling finger began pulling at the restraining sheet trying desperately to release her friend.

Kate's face turned beet red; her eyes rolled back in her head; her mouth opened in an unheard scream. Miss Porter looked at her in alarm and quickly pulled at the sheets. Mary Lou yanked from the opposite side.

"Kate, Kate, it's okay. You're free." Mary Lou covered her friend's trembling body with a blanket.

Kate looked around at her fellow students. She took in a deep breath then looked away. "I'm all right," she mumbled as she climbed down from the cot.

"Miss Stephens, you are excused from this activity," the nervous instructor said, replacing her look of alarm with one of detachment. "You may sit over there and observe."

Kate glowered as she stumbled into her clothes.

"What is your name?" the instructor asked pointing to Mary Lou.

"Mary Louise Hammond," she stammered.

"Take her place, please."

Mary Lou hesitantly undressed and took a deep breath as she climbed onto the cot. Demurely she covered her breasts with her hands, avoiding eye contact with her fellow students.

"Put your hands down," Miss Porter said. "You two," she pointed to Blanche and Carol, "stand on either side of the cot and wrap her, just as I demonstrated."

I'm going to close my eyes and relax, Mary Lou thought. Gosh these sheets are cold. I'm shivering, but I'm not going to struggle; that's when you panic. Just lie still, she told herself. Then I might not even realize I'm restrained. She felt the frigid sheets winding around her body, tighter and tighter. Deep breath, she commanded. Relax. There, it's not so cold now. My teeth have stopped chattering. Now it's getting warm. Don't struggle—relax—relax—getting sleepy—close my eyes ...warm...cozy...like a caterpillar in a cocoon.

In a few moments Mary Lou was asleep and dreaming. This time the dream was more vivid. She could see things in detail, even read the street signs.

Margaret Montague walking down Michigan Avenue...looking out onto the lakeshore. Now walking down Prairie Avenue...large Victorian homes on each side of the street. She staggers...not well...calling the doctor...

Mary Lou heard a voice. "Wake up, Miss Hammond. You've had a nice little nap." She heard the instructor's voice from far away, calling her back to reality, but she didn't want to come back. She wanted to stay in the dream. She opened her eyes as her classmates unwrapped the sheets. Then shook her head. The dream had been so real that she almost expected to find herself in Mrs. Montague's parlor.

Later, when the girls were back in their room, Kate continued to complain about the experience in Hydro. "That Miss Porter, I told her I couldn't stand it and to let me out, but what did she say? 'Relax, dear'." Kate mimicked the woman's nasal speech.

"I got you out as quick as I could," Mary Lou said.

"Yeah, but never again. Now you said you had another dream. Tell me about it and I'll write it in the book."

"It was so real," Mary Lou said, wrapping her arms around herself. "I felt like I was there with that woman. First we were walking down Michigan Avenue. I actually read the street sign. I could see Lake Michigan. But that's not right. You can't see the lake from there. Then we were walking down Prairie Avenue. I could read that street sign, too. I was actually there." She scrunched up her face in a frown and shivered.

"What happened next?" Kate asked scribbling in the book.

"Then we were in her parlor. It looked just like those homes you see in the movies with the gaslights on the walls, the heavy red velvet drapes, the thick carpets, and all those fancy couches and chairs. She was calling for the doctor—something wrong with her. That's when Miss Porter woke me up."

She looked at Kate for a moment. "You know, these dreams are just like a serialized story. Could I be tapping into something in the ethers that happened years ago? I read somewhere that every word spoken is floating around somewhere in space."

Mary Lou had a faraway look in her eyes, as if she were partly in another dimension. Kate looked at her with apprehension. Something strange was happening to her dearest friend. She was frightened; had to talk to someone about it. It certainly didn't seem like this was going to stop.

"You've got an over-active imagination, that's all," she said, trying to convince herself as well as Mary Lou. "I'll bet you saw a movie once about this Mrs. Montague and forgot all about it. Now, for some reason, you're remembering it in bits and pieces. How's that for an explanation?"

"It doesn't wash, Kate. I didn't tell you, but when I was being unwrapped, my silver chain was lying on the sheets, just as though someone had opened the clasp. Every time I have a dream, the necklace comes undone, as though she's trying to tell me that she's real."

"Who's trying to tell you?" Kate almost didn't want to hear the answer.

"Why Margaret Montague, of course."

Chapter 17

Mary Lou wasn't sure she was up to spending a Sunday afternoon in mid-January with Bill, but it did mean getting away from Hillside for a while. She had forgiven him for buying her earrings she couldn't wear. ecided it was an honest mistake. He picked her up at Hillside and, as they drove through the gate, she tried to leave all thoughts of the hospital, the patients, and, especially, Margaret Montague, behind. She promised herself that she wouldn't let anything spoil her day.

He drove to downtown Chicago and parked the car in Grant Park. Hand in hand they walked along Michigan Avenue. The weather was mild for this time of the year: a winter thaw that brought people out onto the streets. They people watched and laughed at nothing in particular like normal young people.

Mary Lou felt free, just being away from the atmosphere of Hillside. It all seemed so far away. She reveled in being here amid life, basking in the winter sunshine.

"How is your paper coming?" she asked. "The one about the Chicago reconstruction period."

"Just fine. It's really fascinating. You know that old Water Tower north of here?"

Mary Lou nodded trying to look interested.

"That was the only building left standing around here after the fire."

"Yes, you told me that. And wasn't Prairie Avenue a very wealthy area at that time?" She envisioned the area, as it was now, old dilapidated houses and high crime rates.

"It sure was. Everybody who was anybody lived there."

"Where was the lakeshore back then?" she asked suddenly remembering her dream.

"As a matter of fact the lakeshore came up almost to where we're standing right now." They stopped and looked east across the avenue and Grant Park. The lake wasn't even visible from where they stood. "Michigan Avenue bordered the lakefront just like Lakeshore Drive does now. Why are you asking?" He gave her a quizzical look.

She shrugged. "No particular reason. I read something somewhere and wanted to be sure I had the facts straight. It said that the wealthy folks strolling down Michigan Avenue could see the lake. Our nurses' home at St. Benedict's is on Prairie Avenue, but we're nowhere near the lake."

"All the area from Michigan Avenue to the lake shore is land fill," Bill said. "I'm not sure how far south they went, but at least up to Roosevelt Road. That was done after the fall of old Prairie Avenue. There was so much industry around that the old mansions were covered in soot. The millionaires started moving north to Michigan Avenue, along what was called the gold coast. The more adventurous ones went all the way to Lake Forest...."

Bill rambled on and on about his favorite subject, old Chicago. Mary Lou pretended to listen, but her mind was elsewhere. She had promised herself to put the dreams out of her mind, at least for today, but they resurfaced, in vivid color. She could almost see Margaret Montague walking just where they were, looking at the lake. So my dream was accurate, she thought. I didn't know anything about the original borders of the lake. So how could my subconscious mind bring up old memories, if there were none? No, this is something else. These dreams are not coming from my subconscious. But from where?

"Mary Lou, are you listening to me?" Bill asked impatiently. "If I'm boring you, just say so."

"I'm sorry. I was distracted for a while, trying to visualize how it must have looked back then."

He looked down at her, "Are you sure you're not having any more of those dreams?" He slid his arm around her and pulled her close. "I'm worried about you. I don't like the way you look; you're pale and have dark circles under your eyes. That makeup doesn't hide anything, either."

"I'm okay, honest." She looked at him and smiled trying to look unconcerned. "I haven't had a dream in ages. By the way, I've been doing research, too. I decided to do my paper on developmental disorders and I think I found out why I can write backwards."

"Why?"

"Well, some researchers think that people who never fully developed a dominant side of the brain have that ability, or disability, whatever you want to call it. I was born left-hand dominant, but my mother forced me to learn the fine motor skills, like writing, with my right hand. I still do a lot of things with my left hand, like cutting, slicing, lifting. Anything that requires strength—there goes lefty."

"Do you feel better now that you found a reason?" Bill asked. "No more worrying, no more paranoia about being mentally unbalanced?"

"Nope. I'm perfectly fine," she lied. "Before I forget," Mary Lou slipped her note in Bill's pocket.

"Did you proofread it this time?" he asked.

"Yes, I did. Nobody's message on it but mine."

Bill didn't believe her one bit. Her appearance belied her words, but he didn't question her. I'll discuss it with Kate, he thought. I'll call her, meet for coffee or something. Then maybe I'll get the truth.

Chapter 18

"Come on gals," Kate called, pacing nervously. "We're not going to the Ritz you know."

"Hold on, we're coming." Blanche and Carol emerged wearing woolen sweaters and skirts, bobby socks, and penny loafers. Tonight was their first dance with the patients and they knew that the recreation hall was drafty.

"I don't really want to do this," Blanche squealed buttoning her coat. "The thought of those people touching me gives me the willies."

"They won't hurt you," Mary Lou said. "Only the harmless ones are allowed at the dances." She wasn't certain about this. She remembered all too clearly her recent experience on 13. But certainly none of those patients would be there.

The night was exceptionally dark with no moonlight to guide them. The buildings looked black and foreboding like a scene from a horror movie. Mary Lou almost expected to see something or someone jump out at them at any moment.

"Stay close together," Kate cautioned. "It's spooky out here."

"Maybe we'll see the ghost," Carol said sliding between Blanche and Kate.

"Don't talk nonsense," Blanche said. "There isn't any ghost, is there?"

"Of course not," Kate said. "Come on, let's get inside." She opened the door to the recreation center and ran in, stamping her feet and blowing on her hands. The others followed.

The room felt as drafty as an old barn. Faded crepe paper streamers hung forlornly in the corners, remnants of some long forgotten festivity. The wooden floor was stained and worn from years of use. A three-piece combo began setting up on the stage.

Josephine came waltzing by with an imaginary partner singing "After the Ball Was Over". She seemed to be in her own world, her scrawny body swaying to music that only she could hear.

Martha Dillard stood with a group of patients, apparently instructing them on the proper procedure for the dance. She was wearing her uniform, regulation shoes, and her nurse's cap.

"Don't you think that for once old Dill Pickle could let her hair down and wear street clothes like a normal person?" Kate asked.

"Maybe she doesn't have any," Blanche whispered.

"Don't be silly," Mary Lou said feeling she had to defend the woman. "She doesn't have to come here on her time off. Look at how protective she is of those patients. She's an authority figure. They might not recognize her if she didn't wear her uniform."

"Look," Kate said pointing. "Isn't that Ben, the doctor? He looks pretty good dressed in a shirt and tie, even if it's crooked. Oh look. 'Dill Pickle' is straightening it for him. Now she's adjusting his belt." Kate's eyebrows rose as she watched the ministrations of her instructor. "Remember how defensive she was when we tried to read *his* chart? She's going to dance with him." She nodded exchanging knowing glances with Mary Lou.

The music started with a simple two-step. Martha Dillard led Ben onto the dance floor and began to lead. He followed her, hesitantly, his eyes staring at nothing. She whispered something in his ear. Was that a hint of a smile on his face? Mary Lou wondered. A few patients danced with each other. Josephine continued her waltz, weaving between the couples. When she came up to Mary Lou and Kate she said in a low singsong voice, "Martha and Ben...Martha and Ben...I know a secret." Then she danced away cackling her unnerving laugh.

The young violinist stood there wiggling his fingers. He looked at Kate and smiled. "Maybe I'll play again. Do you think so?"

"Sure. Come on, let's dance." She led him haltingly out onto the floor. He tripped, stammered and promptly stomped on her foot. She grimaced but continued to dance until the music stopped.

"Thank you," he said wiggling his fingers faster. "Do you really think I'll be able to play again?"

"Sure, kid, sure."

"That was a sweet thing you did," Mary Lou said coming up to her friend.

"He's kind of pitiful. I feel sorry for him. He'll probably spend the rest of his life wiggling his fingers and asking the same question."

A tall heavy-set man walked up to Mary Lou. "Did you know I was conceived in a coca cola bottle?" he asked, a note of authority in his voice.

"No, I didn't," she said. "Uh, do you want to dance?"

"No, thank you. I just wanted you to know about my humble beginning." He walked away and stopped to tell another group of students.

The girls looked at each other, shook their heads, and wondered what would happen next. Attendants busily tried to line up the patients for a dance called London Bridge. Two people held their arms up joining hands to form a bridge. Each couple went under and then formed an extension in front of the previous couple.

The venture started out with some success until someone started pushing. One woman slapped another. The two began shouting obscenities and pulling each other's hair.

The attendants grabbed the transgressors and carted them off before they caused a general panic. Miss Dillard and the other staff members calmed the rest of the patients as the music resumed. Josephine stood in a corner watching and laughing as loud as she could.

"Let's get out of here," Kate said. "I've had enough of this." The others agreed and they slipped out unnoticed into the night.

The moon had disappeared behind a bank of clouds. The girls hurried through the black night.

"What was that?" Carol asked grabbing Mary Lou's arm.

"What?"

"I heard something. Listen."

They stopped and huddled together in silence. A soft moaning sound filled the stiff night air.

"There, I heard it again," Carol said. "Didn't you?" She squeezed Mary Lou's arm tighter.

"Shush."

They heard it again, only louder this time; an unearthly moan that lingered in the air.

"It's the ghost," Blanche whispered.

"Don't be silly, there's no ghost," Kate said.

"Something moved behind that tree," Blanche said. "I'm getting out of here." She turned and ran toward the nurses' residence followed closely by the other three.

Mary Lou looked back for just a moment and thought she saw the animal she and Kate had spotted near the cemetery. Two yellow eyes peered at her through the gloom. She shivered and hurried after the others.

Josephine came out from behind the tree, cackling her insane laughter and dancing around in the snow.

When Mary Lou and Kate opened the door to their room, they stopped and listened.

"What is that music?" Kate asked as she pulled the cord on the light.

Mary Lou felt light-headed when she looked at her music box on the dresser. The figures danced round and round to the "Blue Danube Waltz".

"Did you wind that up before we left?" Kate asked.

"No," Mary Lou whispered. "But who did?"

Chapter 19

The next morning Mary Lou was still shaken from the experience with the music box. She couldn't think of any way it could have happened. Kate just shook it off as some fault in the mechanism.

"I'm not looking forward to today," Kate said as they sat in the dining room. "Mmm, these rolls are delicious."

Mary Lou looked at her with a frown. "Blanche said that Insulin Coma Therapy is pretty bad. The nurses on the night shift give the Insulin, so when we get there the patients should be showing signs of hypoglycemia." She shivered at the thought. "I don't know how long it takes them to go into a coma."

"That's really gruesome," Kate said putting down her roll. "There has to be a better way to treat people with Schizophrenia."

Mary Lou looked out of the curtained window at the snowy world trying to see into the future. "Someday there will be, but not now."

Miss Dillard's authoritative voice filled the dining room. "Those of you scheduled for Insulin Coma Therapy, come with me."

"That's us," Kate said and stuffed the last bite of roll in her mouth.

"Nothing spoils your appetite does it?" Mary Lou asked, shaking her head.

"Nope. Eating is one of the pleasures of life that I don't deny myself."

The girls followed their instructor out into the cold biting air and huddled into the treatment building. The darkened room held six patients separated from one another by flimsy curtains. The students' assignment was to take vital signs and chart their observations. Two registered nurses worked in the room, observing the students and assuming legal responsibility. A doctor made rounds frequently to determine the appropriate time to bring the patients out of the coma.

"How many treatments have these patients had?" Miss Dillard asked the nurse in charge.

"Those in beds one and two have had twenty. Their Insulin dose has been gradually increased. They should be allowed to go into full coma. Beds three and four have had ten. They'll only go into a light comatose state before we give the glucose solution. Beds five and six are having their first treatment. They've been given a low dose of Insulin that is not enough to put them into a comatose state. We'll watch them closely."

Miss Dillard nodded. "Thank you. Each of you has been assigned to one of these patients. Take their vital signs every fifteen minutes. Call the charge nurse as soon as they lose consciousness. I'll be back in a half-hour."

Mary Lou felt the perspiration pooling with the starch of her stiff uniform, trickling down her arm, and making her squirm. She looked at her patient, one of the first timers. As she pumped up the blood pressure cuff, she examined the youthful face. Expressionless hazel eyes stared back at her. Her acne-covered cheeks had a sallow hue. The bow-shaped mouth drooped. Lank mousy brown hair fell across the pillow with none of the luster of health.

This girl can't be any older than I am, Mary Lou thought. She noted the vital signs on the chart: blood pressure 118/70, pulse 88, and respirations 20. She wiped the girl's brow while she kept talking to her, reassuring her that everything would be all right. Does she hear my voice? Does she even know I'm here?

For the next forty-five minutes there was no change in the girl's status. The doctor had made rounds, examined all six patients, and said he would be back in a half-hour to administer the glucose to bring this girl's blood level back to normal. Mary Lou kept talking to her the entire time expecting some response, but the body lay motionless. Only the rise and fall of her chest indicated that she was alive.

Suddenly the girl's eyes rolled back in her head; her body stiffened; she began convulsing.

"Miss Dillard!" Mary Lou screamed as she thrust a padded tongue blade between the girl's teeth. The nurses ran up and surrounded the bed. One of them attempted to pass a large Boas tube down her throat, but her teeth remained tightly clamped on the tongue blade as her body stiffened in another convulsion.

"What happened?" the doctor asked, running back into the room.

"She suddenly started convulsing," the charge nurse said as she kept struggling to get the tube between the girl's teeth.

"Get me a Levine tube!" he shouted looking down at the patient. Quickly he inserted the thinner tube into the girl's nostril in a vain attempt to get it down her throat.

"Damn, she's got a deviated septum. I can't get it through on either side. Phenobarbital, quick. Someone get an IV going. We've got to stop these convulsions."

Perspiration lined his forehead as he injected the barbiturate into the girl's thrashing arm. One of the nurses tried to start an IV drip, but she kept missing the tiny vein under the thin papery skin.

"No good—it's not working. Give me another dose," the harried doctor shouted.

"But Doctor, you've already given her the maximum safe dose," the charge nurse said, her eyes bulging, her hands shaking.

"Well, do you want her to die in Status Epilepticus or of Hypoglycemia?" he asked through gritted teeth.

The nurse quickly drew up another dose. The doctor jabbed it into the patient then turned his attention to starting the IV line.

Miss Dillard pulled the terrified trembling Mary Lou away from the bed as they worked in vain over the frail body that kept thrashing on the bed.

"Miss Dillard, what did I do wrong?" she asked, her voice breaking.

"You did nothing wrong. These things happen." The instructor's voice softened as she led Mary Lou out of the room.

"Her vital signs were stable. Your observations were accurate. The convulsion was an unpredictable complication." She sighed and shook her head. "Sometimes we don't have complete histories on these patients. I'm sure if we did, we would find that she's had seizures before. That would have been a contraindication for this type of therapy."

"Will she be all right?" Mary Lou asked gripping her hands tightly.

Martha Dillard looked away, out the window and across the huge expanse of snow, her face a mask. "Probably not." She shook her head. "It's a common problem," she continued, whether talking to Mary Lou or to herself. "No family, no history, doctors and nurses working with meager information and inadequate staff." She turned back to Mary Lou. "It's no one's fault, so don't blame yourself."

Mary Lou glanced back into the room just as the doctor pulled the sheet over the girl's face. She gasped.

Miss Dillard pulled her away. "You're excused for the rest of the morning. Go back to the nurses' home and lie down."

Mary Lou grabbed her coat and hat and ran out of the building blinded by tears. She wasn't sure just where she was going, just felt the need to run. Suddenly she collided with someone.

"Uh," she muttered. Then looked up into the smiling face of Dr. Corbett.

"And where are you going in such a hurry?" he asked, grabbing her arms to steady her. "What's wrong? Why are you crying?"

"I have to get away from here," she said between sobs. She felt her whole body shaking.

"Easy, easy. Whatever happened can't be as bad as all that," he said, a soothing tone to his voice. "Come on, let's get a cup of hot chocolate and you can tell me all about it."

She didn't argue, didn't pull away, just let him take her arm and lead her along. When she realized they were at the dining room, she looked at him, a question in her eyes. "But they aren't serving now."

He winked. "If you know the right people, you can get coffee or hot chocolate at any time." He took her hand and led her through the empty room, the tables set up for lunch. He went straight into the kitchen.

"Agnes, are you here?" he called.

"Who is it?" a sharp accented voice called back. A heavy-set woman wearing a stained white apron over her cotton dress and a white scarf around her gray hair looked at them. Her frown turned into a welcoming smile.

"Where have you been you naughty boy? Why don't you come to see old Agnes, huh?"

He gave her a contrite look pulling down the sides of his mouth. "They work me too hard here," he said in a little boy voice.

"Shame. Look how skinny you are. And who is this girl? Did you make her cry?"

Mary Lou hastily wiped the tears from her face.

"You know I wouldn't do that, Agnes. Now, she's had a bad experience on the ward and desperately needs a cup of your special hot chocolate."

"Good you bring her here. Sit over there in my kitchen and warm up. I bring you chocolate." She motioned to a small metal table in the corner flanked by two wooden chairs.

"Thanks, beautiful. You're the best," he said caressing the woman's flabby cheek.

"Go on, go on. Sit. Sit. I make the chocolate." She bustled away looking back and smiling.

He led Mary Lou to the table, held out a chair for her, and then occupied the other. They took off their coats and let them drape over the backs of the chairs.

"Now, do you want to tell me what happened?" he asked.

Mary Lou sighed, rubbed her face, sat back in the chair and closed her eyes for a moment. "I was assigned to assist with Insulin Coma Therapy. My patient was a young girl getting her first treatment..." She slowly told him what happened, then looked into his face.

He gritted his teeth, frowned, and shook his head. "That's exactly what I objected to when the great Dr. Forester gave his lecture on the *state of the art* treatment for mental illness. Those patients can aspirate their own saliva and get pneumonia, not to mention the possibility of heart failure. It makes me furious that we're still in the Dark Ages in psychiatry."

At that moment Agnes came up to them with a tray holding two steaming mugs and a plate of cookies. "You too serious. No shop talk. Tell this girl how pretty she is." She winked at Mary Lou, gave the young doctor a tweak to his chin and walked away.

"She's a great gal," he said taking a sip of chocolate.

"Is she a patient?" Mary Lou asked.

"No, her husband is. She works here to be near him."

"Will he ever be released?"

"I doubt it. He's manic-depressive, tried to commit suicide a couple of times. Recently he's developed Parkinson's. I think this will be his home for the rest of his life. Agnes can't care for him so she rented an apartment in the area for convenience. This place is her world." He shook his head.

"That's so sad," Mary Lou said.

"It's life, my dear. Now drink your chocolate. She has her own recipe, for special people." He smiled, winked at her and took another sip.

"This is great," Mary Lou said savoring the sweet taste. "I feel better already. How can I thank you for being so understanding, Dr. Corbett?"

"Hey, my father is Dr. Corbett. Call me Jack. And you are Mary?"

"Mary Lou."

"I like Mary better. It was my mother's name. Do you mind if I call you that?"

"Not at all." She liked the way it sounded when he said the name. She took another sip of chocolate and reached for a cookie. It melted in her mouth with the first bite. "Delicious."

After she finished the chocolate and two more cookies, Mary Lou sat back and sighed.

"Feeling better?" he asked.

"Much. You said your father is Dr. Corbett. What field is he in?"

Jack frowned. "Psychiatry. He's expecting me to go into practice with him when I finish my residency."

"Don't you want to?"

"The more I see around here, the more disillusioned I become with the field." He pushed his empty cup aside and leaned his arms on the table. "I'm seriously thinking of going into research. I have another year here. In my spare time I've been studying the chemistry of the brain, at least as much as we know about it today. I'd like to be one of the pioneers in finding new drugs to change brain chemistry and alter behavior. Then we won't have to kill people with electrodes and Insulin."

Mary Lou cringed as the memory of her experience surfaced.

"What about you, Mary? What do you intend to do after you graduate?"

"I really haven't given it much thought. We graduate in June, take State Board Exams in the summer, and then?" She shrugged.

"You have plenty of time." He looked at his watch. "Now I must get over to the men's violent ward. I'm supposed to see a patient there who refuses to eat."

"Thanks, Jack, for taking time with me. I appreciate it."

They thanked Agnes for the goodies and left the dining room.

"You'll be okay?" he asked.

"Sure, I'll be fine."

As she walked back to her room, Mary Lou kept going over their conversation. He sure was a nice guy, and so attentive. She found herself comparing him with Bill. Wasn't that disloyal? No, she thought, he's just—different She decided not to share this experience with Kate, at least, not yet. For now, she would remember it and savor it, tuck it away into a special corner of her mind.

That night Mary Lou tossed and turned, unable to sleep. Her talk with Jack had helped temporarily. But now it all came back. She went over the entire scene again in her mind, step by step. But there was nothing she could have changed. What a wasted life. What kind of life did that girl have? I didn't even know her name, she thought. Somehow that made it all the worse. She fantasized about who the girl might have been, what kind of things she liked to do, what was important to her, tried to make her real, but all she could see were the staring eyes, the acne-covered face, the lank hair. She wasn't real at all, just an illusion.

Finally Mary Lou turned on the light and decided to study. She looked over at Kate, fast asleep. She shook her head. Maybe if I keep my mind busy, I'll be able to forget, to relax a little. She turned to the chapter on schizophrenia and began to read, but she couldn't concentrate. She read the same paragraph over and over but remembered nothing. She made a few notes, but soon became groggy. Without realizing it, she took the pencil in her left hand and began to write a mirror-image message.

I have been trying to make contact
all these years.
I have finally succeeded.
Do not fail me.
MM

The paper and pencil slid off the bed onto the floor as Mary Lou fell into a fitful sleep. She began to dream, but this time the dream appeared in even more vivid detail. The conversation was more intimidating.

A four poster bed...windows from floor to ceiling...lace curtains flanked by heavy velvet draperies...a figure lying on the bed....

In a corner three people talking in whispered tones. "Acute depression, common in women her age—continue barbiturates...."
Another voice..."forgetting important dates... embarrassing...."
A man and woman embrace each other. The figure on the bed looks at them and screams..."cut...you...off...see...banker tomorrow"....

In the morning Kate took in the scene: Mary Lou's disheveled bed, books and papers on the floor. She knew what kind of night she had. She walked over to straighten the covers and saw the note on the floor. She winced as she held it up to the mirror and read it. Deciding it would be better to hide it, she tucked it into the notebook where they catalogued all the dreams and wondered how this was all going to end.

Chapter 20

For the next few days clouds obscured the sun casting a dreary gloom over the entire complex. A freezing rain fell continuously adding to the bleakness. Mary Lou was overcome by a feeling of hopelessness.

Kate had written down the dream in the notebook exactly as Mary Lou remembered it. She thought about telling her of the most recent note, but didn't think her friend could handle any more right now.

"I can't get that poor epileptic girl out of my mind," Mary Lou said. "I didn't even know her name." She lay on her bed staring at the ceiling.

"Would it have made a difference if you had?" asked Kate. "Lulu you have to stop brooding. There's nothing anyone could have done about it. They tried every- thing. It was her time, that's all."

"Do you really believe that?" Mary Lou asked sitting up in bed. "Do you think that we all have a time to die, no matter what anyone does?" She slowly shook her head trying to decide whether she believed it or not.

Kate shrugged. "Sometimes it seems to be the only explanation. One person might be the only survivor of a terrible accident. By all the odds, that person should have died with the rest. Why didn't he?" She looked at her roommate. "You know, I remember in our first year of nurses' training something weird happened. I admitted a young woman who was going to have a simple D and C. That's really routine, you know. That morning, when I got her ready for surgery, she told me she was going to die. She was so scared."

Mary Lou sat forward on the bed listening to Kate's every word. "What happened?"

"Well, I said all the usual things to calm her down. This is a simple procedure, takes about a half-hour. No one dies from it."

Kate looked out the window as if she were reliving the experience. "But she *did* die, from the anesthesia," she whispered. Then she looked back at Mary Lou. "How did she know? A premonition? Was it her time? Sometimes I really do believe that."

"When did you become a philosopher?" Mary Lou asked. "Usually all you talk about is food and guys." Mary Lou shrugged. "Maybe you're right. I just can't stop thinking about that girl." I wonder if Margaret Montague knew when it was her time? She thought. God, I have to stop fantasizing about that woman. She probably exists only in my mind.

"Kate, phone call." They heard Blanche's voice outside the door.

"Coming," Kate called back. "That'll be my mom," she said walking to the door. "I haven't talked to her in two weeks. She's probably wondering if I'm still a resident of planet Earth."

When Kate walked into the hallway Blanche stood there grinning. "It's a guy," she whispered rolling her eyes.

"A guy? Probably my brother."

Kate hurried to the phone wondering if there was a problem at home. Her brother never called her.

"Hello," she said.

"Kate, this is Bill."

She was surprised at the sound of his voice. "Gosh, this must be mental telepathy or something. I've been meaning to call you."

"I'm worried about Mary Lou," he said. "She's acting so strange. And she looks terrible, like she's not sleeping."

"You're right, she's isn't. I'm worried, too. She hasn't told you, but she's still having those dreams and they're getting more detailed. Listen, we can't talk about this over the phone. Somebody's behind me waiting to make a call."

"Can you meet me Friday night for a cup of coffee?" Bill asked. "That restaurant about a block east of the hospital? Say seven o'clock?"

"Okay. Then maybe we can come up with some ideas. And I'll bring the notebook with the dreams." Kate walked slowly back to the room deciding what to tell her friend.

"Was it your mom?" Mary Lou asked.

"Yeah, she wanted to know everything that's going on."

"You didn't talk very long?" Mary Lou looked at the clock.

"Uh, no. Sarah had to make an important call. I told Mom I'd write her a long letter. I'd better get to it."

The next morning dawned sunny and bright. Mary Lou woke refreshed from a dreamless sleep. She even felt better. *I really have to put everything in perspective. Today is a new day; the only day I have control over. Yesterday has already happened and tomorrow is yet to come. So, I must concentrate on today.* She had read that somewhere, didn't remember where, but it was good advice.

"Kate, get up. It's time for breakfast. Then we're going to learn about tertiary syphilis."

"Huh?" Kate moaned as she turned over in bed. "That's just what I always wanted to know." She grunted then sat up and blew out a long breath. "You're chipper today. What's up?" She squinted at her roommate.

"I feel pretty good, for a change." She smiled. "Let's go learn all about the disease that killed Al Capone."

Miss Dillard stood before the class. She looked visibly drawn, dark rings circled her eyes, her face an unreadable mask. She caught Mary Lou's eye for just a moment. The girl felt concern coming from her instructor, but, just as quickly, the moment passed and Miss Dillard began the lecture.

"Today's lesson is on syphilis, actually, neurosyphilis, to be exact. This is the third stage of the disease. The first stage is the chancre; a generalized rash, malaise and fever characterize the second stage. The disease can be treated at these two stages. But, many times, milder cases go undiagnosed. No one wants to admit to having venereal disease." She looked around at the students most of them furiously taking notes. Then she looked out the window again, back to the class, and resumed her lecture.

"The organism, *treponema pallidum* can lie dormant in the body for as long as fifteen to twenty years. Then it invades the central nervous system where damage is irreversible. The symptoms are those of *tabes* and *paresis*."

Mary Lou made sure she wrote down the name of the organism and the symptoms of the third stage. Miss Dillard always asked detailed questions on the exams.

"Miss Dillard," Blanche asked. "What are *tabes* and *paresis*?"

"I'll get to that in a moment." She frowned at Blanche. "If you had read the chapter in preparation for today's lecture, Miss Andrews, you would be familiar with the terms."

Blanche shrunk down in her seat as the instructor frowned at her.

Carol giggled.

Miss Dillard took a deep breath, and continued. "When the organism invades the central nervous system, the disease is known as neurosyphilis."

Mary Lou underlined that statement. The emphasis in Miss Dillard's voice said it was sure to be on a test.

"*Paresis* presents with symptoms of chronic dementia: such as memory loss, impaired intellect, personality changes, defects in judgment, delusions, and inappropriate behavior. Many of these patients have delusions of grandeur, claiming to be Julius Caesar, Cleopatra, or other famous people. You'll see them on the wards. One fellow walks around blessing everyone and forgiving sins. He claims to be the Pope." She stopped for a moment. A rare smile crossed her face, but she quickly resumed her demeanor of superiority.

"This stage lasts four or five years. The patients gradually deteriorate until they die. Arsenic compounds sometimes arrest the disease, but at the present, there is no known treatment. Does anyone have any questions?"

"If this is a physical problem, why are these patients in a psychiatric hospital?" someone asked.

"Because the disease causes deterioration with mental problems. In years to come we won't see this stage anymore. With the advent of penicillin, the disease is totally curable in the first stage. Within the next fifteen to twenty years there will be no cases of tertiary syphilis. Public education will alert the population to early treatment and prevention." She looked around at the students and, again, her eyes rested on Mary Lou for just a moment, then she resumed.

"A few words about *tabes dorsalis*. This affects the gait, balance and vision. Patients have difficulty walking. You'll see them on the ward slapping their feet as they walk. They lose the reflexes in the feet and knees until they become totally incapacitated. Are there any more questions?" Her look dared anyone else to ask a question.

"All right then, let's go to the wards."

They followed the instructor out into the bright sunshine. Something about the late January day said that spring would be early that year. Mary Lou walked with a lighter step as she followed the others.

"Mary Lou," Sarah called. "You dropped something in the snow. Right there, see? It's something shiny."

Mary Lou bent down to look, but she knew what it was, her silver chain. The clap was open. Tightness clutched at her chest. Margaret Montague wasn't finished with her yet.

As she looked up a skinny figure clad in a black cape came into view. Josephine danced through the snow as she approached Mary Lou.

"I know a secret. I know a secret," she said in her whiny voice.

"What's the secret?" Mary Lou asked in a whisper.

"Flowers in the cemetery," Josephine whispered back.

"Who puts them there? Can you tell me that?"

"Ask Miss Dillard. She knows... she knows...." Josephine's cackle filled the air as she sprinted through the snow. Her cape flew open; a long scarf sailed behind her; her feet sank into the snow up to her bare ankles.

Mary Lou frowned. Sure I'll ask Miss Dillard, and she'll tell me to mind my own business, she thought.

Chapter 21

"The way I see it," Kate said when Mary Lou told her what Josephine had said, "Dill Pickle must be putting those flowers in the cemetery herself."

"She seems the most unlikely person to be putting flowers anywhere," Mary Lou said. Then she remembered the single red rose on the instructor's desk.

"Pass me another roll, will you, Lulu? These are super tonight."

"You are an absolute glutton. Here, take the last one. By the way, did you talk to that patient on the ward who thought he was a millionaire? He's really strange. He wrote out a check for Blanche."

"I didn't see that. What kind of a check? Was it for real?"

"Of course not. He took a piece of paper and started writing across the page. Then he turned it and wrote down the side. He kept turning the paper and writing in a circle. The words kept getting smaller and smaller. When he got to the center, you couldn't read it."

"What did it say?"

"Every filthy and obscene word I've ever seen and a lot more that I didn't recognize. I'm sure he made some of them up. The staff said he gets his kicks out of shocking the students. He just walks up to anyone new and says, 'Did I give you a check?' When the person says no, he gets busy with his pencil and paper. He's a funny old coot." Mary Lou laughed remembering the small, wizened man with only a few hairs sticking up on his head. His knobby fingers curled into claws so that he could barely hold the pencil.

"Then there was a woman talking to one of the new interns. She had on an inch of makeup, false eyelashes, the whole bit. When he asked her name she became very indignant. She said anyone could see that she was Rita Hayworth."

"That's really delusions of grandeur," Kate said finishing the roll. "But let's get back to Josephine."

"Why? She's not a reliable source of information," Mary Lou said.

"But she's the only source we've got. I'd like to grab her around her scrawny neck and shake the truth out of her," Kate said.

"Now you're getting vicious. She'd only whine and cry and probably make up some outlandish story."

"Why don't we try bribing her?" Kate asked, her eyes lighting up. "She loves chocolate. We can use that."

"I haven't seen any around this place," Mary Lou said. "We'll have to buy some."

Kate scraped the last bite of apple pie off her plate. "Ugh, I'm stuffed. Let's take a walk."

"You should be stuffed. You ate like a pig. Honestly, you're beginning to bulge around the middle."

The girls bundled up against the brisk evening cold. A full moon cast a bright cheerless light over the landscape. They decided to walk to the drugstore two blocks away and get some chocolate bars with the promise that Kate wouldn't eat them.

"What are you doing this weekend?" Mary Lou asked.

"Nothing much," Kate answered nervously. "You're going home, aren't you?"

"I was planning to, but I changed my mind. I think I'll stay here and finish my paper."

"But it's not due for two more weeks," Kate whined. "You're always so efficient."

"If I finish it this weekend, then next weekend I can go to Bill's house. His sister, Lydia, is taking a typing course. She said she needs the practice and will type it for me."

"Oh." Kate didn't know what to say. She had planned on Mary Lou being gone so she and Bill would have some time to talk about the problems and maybe come up with a solution. Now she would have to make excuses. I'm such a lousy liar. What can I say? I'll have to come up with something that sounds convincing. She hesitated for a minute.

"Since you said you'd be going home, I asked Blanche and Carol to go to the movies Friday night. Maybe you want to come along? It's not definite though." Maybe Bill and I will have to cancel our meeting, she thought, but I hope not. She seems better, but it might not last.

"Penny for your thoughts, Kate," Mary Lou said.

"A penny. I insist on a check for a million dollars. Nothing less will do."

The girls began to laugh as they neared the drug store. Then stopped suddenly. They saw a familiar figure walking toward them.

"Lulu, look. It's Dill Pickle and aren't those flowers she's carrying?"

"Good evening, Miss Dillard," they said in unison.

Martha Dillard stopped suddenly, visibly surprised. "Oh, good evening." She held the flowers close to her body, cradling them in her arms. "Where are you two going?"

"Just to the drug store. We needed a walk after that great supper tonight," Kate said staring at the bouquet.

"Oh, I see. Don't walk too far. It's quite cold tonight." She hurried past them trying to conceal the flowers.

The girls slipped into the warm drug store. The night was colder than they thought. "Now isn't that strange," Kate said pursing her lips and raising her eyebrows. "Who goes out in the middle of winter on a frigid night to buy flowers?"

Mary Lou picked up two candy bars, one light chocolate and one dark. As she opened her purse, she asked the clerk, "Is there a florist shop around here?"

"Sure, about a half a block down, but they close at six thirty. If you hurry you can just make it."

"Thanks," Mary Lou said.

"You're a sly one," Kate said as they hurried out of the store.

The girls began to run down the slushy sidewalk, slipping and sliding as they went. They could see the lights still on in the small florist shop ahead.

"What are we going to say?" Mary Lou asked, panting.

118 Helen Macie Osterman

"Leave it to me," Kate answered as she opened the door.

"I was just about to close, ladies," the proprietor said. "Did you want something special?"

"No, I just wanted to price the roses. Next week is my mother's birthday and I wondered if I can afford to send her a dozen." Kate smiled innocently.

The florist shook his head. "Roses are always expensive in the winter and they're not worth the money. Now I suggest a bouquet of red carnations with baby's breath. That makes up real nice."

"That sound good," Kate said. "By the way, we just saw one of our instructors coming out of here with flowers." She gave him her most disarming smile.

"You mean Miss Dillard? You girls' students at Hillside? I suspected that you were. Miss Dillard's one of my regular customers. She loves flowers. Every month she comes in and buys three pink carnations and some baby's breath. Always the same. I guess she likes pink. One day I ran out and she was real upset. I tried to give her white ones but she said they had to be pink. Since then I always keep a supply on hand. She comes in like clockwork at the full moon. Yep, a real steady customer."

"Thanks for the information, about my mom's birthday, I mean," Kate stammered.

"I'll think about it and be back. Bye."

They hurried out the door. "Come on Lulu, we've got no time to lose," Kate said starting to run.

"What do you mean?" Mary Lou asked, trying to keep up with her.

"Wanna bet she goes right to the cemetery with those flowers? Think back. What kind of flowers did we see on that little grave? Weren't they pink?"

"You're right, they were pink. And they were carnations. Let's hurry."

The girls ran along the shoveled sidewalks back to Hillside.

Kate began to take deep breaths. Her steps were slowing. "I ate too much. Can't keep running."

Mary Lou agreed. She, too, was beginning to tire. They slowed their pace to a comfortable jog, but it didn't take long for Kate to catch her breath. "We'd better hurry or we'll miss her." She ran on ahead while Mary Lou lagged behind.

When Mary Lou reached the gates, she lost sight of her friend. She continued her jog around the chapel, the power plant, and toward the cemetery. Suddenly a heart-rending cry rent the air. It sent a chill through her. My God, she thought. One of the patients must have gotten out. She looked around and saw Miss Dillard running toward the nurses' home. Then she spotted Kate, walking slowly away from the cemetery. She hurried toward her.

"What happened? Was that Dillard screaming like a banshee? Your face is a white as this snow. What is it?"

"It was so weird," Kate said. "When I got there I saw Dill Pickle inside the cemetery. She must have a key to the gate. She was standing under the oak tree, next to the little white cross. She was talking to somebody, but there was no one there that I could see. It was almost like she was talking to the grave. It sent shivers up my spine. And right beside her sat some sort of animal. I think it was a big cat. Remember the animal we've been seeing lately?"

Mary Lou nodded, shivering.

"It looked at me with glossy yellow eyes. It had long pointed ears, like those cats you see in pictures of Egyptian tombs."

"Are you making this up?" Mary Lou asked, unsure of whether she should believe Kate.

"Honest to God. That's what I saw." Kate crossed her fingers over her heart.

Mary Lou shook her head. "Did she see you?"

"Not right away. I tried to stay in the shadows. It was okay while the moon was behind a cloud. I crouched down and got as close as I could to hear what she was saying." Kate rubbed her eyes. "I shouldn't have been there. It was something very private between her and whoever or whatever is buried there."

The girls walked slowly back to the nurses' residence. "Why did she scream like that?" Mary Lou asked.

"After she put the flowers on the grave she looked up. That's when she saw me and screamed."

"Did she recognize you?" Mary Lou asked, a worried tone to her voice.

"I don't think so. She was so surprised, she just ran. She didn't even stop to lock the gate. I really feel lousy about it." Kate looked down at the ground.

"Me, too. From now on let's stay away from that cemetery and stop asking questions. It's none of our business."

"Another thing," Kate said. "She was crying. Miss Dillard was crying."

"Gosh, she must have a really painful secret. I feel kind of sorry for her," Mary Lou said. She felt ashamed that they had invaded the woman's privacy. They had no right.

"Me, too," Kate agreed.

That night Mary Lou thought about what had happened. There were so many secrets buried in that cemetery. I wish I could forget all about them, she thought: Martha Dillard, the tiny grave, and Margaret Montague. Suddenly she realized she hadn't dreamt about the woman all week. Maybe it's over. Maybe I won't have those dreams anymore. Then she frowned, remembering her necklace falling into the snow, and the music box playing with no one winding it. These seemed to be Margaret Montague's way of reminding her. Reminding her of what? What does she want from me? Mary Lou almost shouted the words out loud. I can't help someone who's been dead for forty years.

She buried her head in the pillow and cried tears of frustration and helplessness. She had to talk about this to someone, but who?

She finally gave up all thoughts of sleep and turned on the light. She looked at Kate fast asleep. Mary Lou listened to her even breathing and sighed. If only I could sleep that way. Maybe if I read a while I'll be able to relax. She picked up a magazine that one of the other students had left behind. For a while the glossy pictures of glamorous models and handsome men held her attention, but soon her eyes felt heavy. Without realizing what she was doing, she took the pencil in her left hand and began to write. Then she fell into a fitful sleep visited by more disassociated dreams.

Chapter 22

A wet snow pelted the windows. Kate woke to see her roommate tossing in her sleep and muttering. Books and papers lay on the floor haphazardly. She had a bad night again, Kate thought. Poor Lulu. I hope Bill has some ideas, because I sure don't.

She slipped into her heavy robe. The cold floor chilled her bare feet; winter winds snaked through the window sashes. Where are my slippers? Kate asked herself. As she looked under the bed she spotted a note lying on the floor. Hesitatingly she picked it up and looked at the mirror-image writing. "Not another one of these," she moaned half aloud. She stuffed her feet into her fuzzy slippers and shuffled to the mirror. For a moment she thought of simply throwing it away without reading it. No, that wouldn't help her friend. She turned on the bedside lamp. Then glanced back at the still sleeping Mary Lou.

As Kate held the note up to the mirror, the message jolted her awake.

Now that I have made contact,
you must help me!
I'll tell you how, soon.
M M

"Damn," Kate said. She thought for a moment, glanced at Mary Lou, and then decided not to show her this note either. She put it in her jacket pocket; she would show it to Bill with the other one she had hidden. She looked down at the sleeping girl, mumbling something incomprehensible. She looked so vulnerable. Kate was afraid for her, really afraid.

"Lulu," she said gently shaking her shoulder. "Lulu, it's time to get up."

Mary Lou sat up with a start, wide eyed and frightened.

"Oh Kate." She reached out her arms. Kate sat down on the bed and put her arms around her friend, rocking her back and forth.

"It's okay, I'm here."

"I had another dream."

"I know," Kate said. "Don't be afraid. Tell me about it and we'll write it in the book."

"It was the same old Victorian house and the same woman. But she looked sick: like she was dying or something. It wasn't as clear as the other ones." Mary Lou looked confused as she tried to recall more of the dream. "That's all I remember." She looked at Kate with a helpless expression, her face a mask of worry and fear.

"It's okay," Kate said, "everything will be all right." But she wasn't so sure about that at all.

Mary Lou fumbled through the day. Her mind wasn't on her work but on the dreams. Mentally she reviewed the entire scenario. There definitely seemed to be a sequence: the wealthy matron, her unfaithful husband, and the implied plot against her. She found herself morbidly wondering what would happen next.

My God, she thought. Am I making up this whole story? It's possible. Here I am waiting for the next episode like a serial at the movies. It's this place. It must be having an effect on my sub-conscious mind. That has to be it. There is no Margaret Montague— there never was. She's a figment of my imagination. Look at history. Why, some people were able to produce the wounds of Christ, the stigmata, through the power of their own minds. That has to be the answer. My mind is telling me a story. I always made up stories in my head when I was a kid. So what am I getting so upset about? I'm sure it will all stop as soon as I get out of here. Only a few more weeks out of an entire lifetime. So how important can it be? After she rationalized her fears, she felt a little better.

"Miss Hammond, Miss Hammond. It's time for you to go off duty. All your classmates have already left. They were looking for you and here you are daydreaming." The charge nurse walked up to her and looked outside. "What are you looking at so intently out that window? Is there something there?"

"It's nothing, Miss Turner. I was daydreaming, just like you said. I'm sorry." She gave the woman a weak smile, grabbed her coat and ran outside.

The wind whipped at her face. She tried to wind her scarf around her neck, but it kept blowing out of her hands. Darn it. As she bent over to pick it up from the ground, Mary Lou noticed a shiny object nestled in the folds of the navy blue wool. She didn't have to wonder what it was. She knew—her silver chain. Margaret Montague was trying to tell her that she *was* real, and not a figment of anyone's imagination. Maybe I should talk to Dr. Corbett, she thought. If this doesn't stop pretty soon, I will. She trudged back to the nurses' home clutching the chain in her hand. I'm going to put this away, she promised herself. I won't wear it again until I leave here.

Kate paced back and forth, her hands gripped into fists. She wondered where Mary Lou was. I'm such a lousy liar, she thought. Lulu is sure to catch me at something. She reviewed her plan. Blanche and some of the other girls were going to the movies. Kate was to go along. They had asked Mary Lou to go, but she said she wanted to stay and work. That sounded logical. What if she changes her mind? Kate wondered. That'll blow the whole thing. Kate had taken Blanche partially into her confidence. She thought back over their conversation.

"Blanche, I need to ask you for a favor."

"Sure, as long as it doesn't involve money. I'm broke."

Kate laughed. "Aren't we all. No, it's not money. I want you to pretend that I'm going to the movies with you in case Lulu asks. You see, uh, Bill is planning a surprise party for her for when we get out of here. Nothing big."

Blanche looked at Kate, and wrinkled her nose. "Yeah?"

"Well, he wants me to help him. So we're meeting tonight to plan the whole thing."

"So you don't want Mary Lou to know you've got a date with her boy friend, huh?" Blanche's eyes gleamed mischievously.

"It's not a date, Blanche. Not that kind of thing. We're going to plan the party, okay?"

"Okay. It's no skin off my nose if you're going out with Mary Lou's guy." She shrugged and held up her hands.

Blanche could be so exasperating at times. She loved to tease, but she could keep a secret. "Another thing," Kate said. "You've got to tell me what the movie's about, so, in case she asks, I'll know."

"Real cloak and dagger stuff, huh? Okay, but you owe me."

"Yeah, I owe you."

They planned that Kate would walk out with Blanche and the others. They would separate at the corner. Kate would go to the restaurant while the others went on to the movie theater.

It should work out all right, Kate thought, unless Lulu changes her mind and decides to go along. I can't worry about that now: one step at a time.

A little later Mary Lou walked into the room and threw herself on the bed. She pulled her knees up to her chest, flexed her elbows and clenched her fists under her chin in the fetal position. Kate stared. "What is it? What are you holding in your hand?"

Mary Lou didn't answer for a long time. With a sad and hopeless expression on her face, she sat up and looked at her friend. "Can't you guess?" she whispered opening her fist to show Kate the shiny chain.

Kate shook her head and sat down beside her.

"Margaret Montague pulled it off again. Just when I had myself convinced that she was a figment of my imagination. She's driving me crazy. I'm obsessed with the woman. I find myself wondering what will happen to her next." Mary Lou trembled as she lay back on the bed.

Kate wanted to cry as she looked at her friend. "You've got to snap out of this," she pleaded. "In a few weeks this will all be over and we'll be out of here. Come on, Lulu." Kate sighed in frustration.

"I'm trying, really I am," Mary Lou said. "Here, please take this chain and lock it in your jewelry box. I don't want her to plague me with it anymore."

Kate took the chain and put it in a separate compartment of her jewelry box, closed the cover and locked it with a tiny gold key. Then she put the key in a small vase on top of the box.

She looked at Mary Lou and was overcome with guilt: both at leaving her and at lying to her. "Will you be all right here alone tonight? Are you sure you don't want to come to the movies?"

Mary Lou shook her head. "I'm not in the mood. I'll be fine. Don't worry. I'm going to try and finish this paper. What movie are you going to see anyway?"

"What movie?" Kate hadn't thought of that. "I don't remember the name, but Blanche said it's supposed to be good."

"Tell me all about it tomorrow. Bye Kate."

"I will, bye." Kate took a deep breath as she closed the door behind her. I almost blew that. Why didn't I ask Blanche the name of the movie? I'm such a klutz. I've got to remember to ask her all about it.

Mary Lou lay on the bed for a while unable to think about working on the paper. She took some deep breaths trying to relax her tense muscles.

"Miss Stephens," Mrs. Dobins called. "You have a phone call."

Mary Lou pulled herself off the bed, dragging one foot after the other. Even opening the door was an effort. "She's not here, Mrs. Dobins," she called.

"It's long distance."

"I'll take it for her. It might be important." She stumbled to the phone and picked up the receiver. It felt so heavy in her hand.

"Hello, this is Mary Lou, Kate's roommate. She's gone out for the evening."

"Oh hello, Mary Lou." Mrs. Stephens' pleasant voice came through the phone. "I just wanted to know how everything is going. I haven't spoken with Kate in weeks."

"But she just talked to you the other day. Didn't you call here?"

"No, dear. I've been out of town. In fact, I'm calling from Denver. I'll be home tomorrow. Tell Kate I'll call her then. I want to tell her all about my trip." Mrs. Stephens hesitated for a moment. "Are you all right? Your voice sounds strained."

"I'm okay, just working too hard."

"Well take care of yourself. You'll soon be home. Goodbye."

Mary Lou felt disoriented as she hung up the phone. Now what? I could have sworn that Kate said her mother called the other day. Did I imagine that, too? No, I distinctly remember her saying she couldn't talk long because someone wanted the phone. Why would she lie to me? I'll ask her when she gets back.

Wearily she walked to the window and looked out. Against the dark night she saw someone looking at her. Startled, she stepped back. Then she realized that it was her own reflection in the glass. "Are you my left-handed friend from the mirror?" She put her hand on the window trying to grasp the other girl's hand. "I've missed you."

For a moment the face appeared to smile. Then a sudden gust of wind blew a cloud of swirling snow across the window obliterating the image.

Mary Lou shuddered. "Oh God, am I really losing my mind?" She remembered a girl named Pauline during their first year of training: a beautiful girl with long dark brown braids wound around the sides of her head. One day Pauline had seen little green men walking across her bed. She left and never returned. Is she locked away in a place like this? Is that my fate, too?

Chapter 23

Bill tapped his fingers nervously on the table. He was on his third cup of coffee. Where is Kate, he wondered? He knew he was early, but she should be here by now. He looked at his watch. How can we possibly help Mary Lou? He asked himself. I don't know anything about psychology. I do know that she's impressionable and that place would give, even a strong person nightmares. But her classmates seem to be handling it. What's wrong with her? I think she needs to see a doctor. I'll suggest that to Kate. He drummed his fingers on the table. When he looked up he saw Kate slinking into the restaurant.

"Kate," Bill called, "over here."

She hurried to the small booth in the corner. "This is just like in the movies, isn't it? I feel like a spy or something." She slid into the seat as far back as possible and looked around as if expecting to see someone she knew.

"What'll you have?" the waitress asked coming up to them.

Kate hesitated for a moment then said, "A cup of hot chocolate, please."

The waitress looked at Bill quizzically. He knew what she was thinking. He usually came in with Mary Lou. Smiling at him, the waitress winked. Bill pretended not to notice. He was definitely uncomfortable being here with Kate. He hoped the waitress wouldn't say anything the next time he came here with Mary Lou. This wasn't such a good idea. They should have gone somewhere else.

"And you, sir?"

"I still have some coffee. No, thanks."

As soon as the waitress left, Kate took out the notebook. "Here's a record of all the dreams. We've been writing them down. There seems to be a definite sequence, like a serialized story. See what you make of it."

Bill read the log slowly, his brows knit in concentration. He put the notebook down when the waitress returned with the chocolate and placed it before Kate.

"Will there be anything else?" she asked, again looking at Bill.

"No thanks," he said and turned back to the notes. "So that's why Mary Lou asked me about the lakefront," His brow furrowed as he read on.

"What?" Kate asked sipping her chocolate.

"When we were downtown she asked about the original shoreline of Lake Michigan. Now I see it had to do with the dreams." He blew out a breath and shook his head.

"Is there any way you can look up this person, this Margaret Montague?" Kate asked. "In some kind of documents or maybe find her birth certificate?"

"Do you have any idea what you're asking? I doubt that there's a social register dating back to the turn of the century." Bill frowned as he thought about it.

"It was the only thing I could think of," Kate said wiping the chocolate from her mouth. "I thought that if we could prove that there was such a person, Lulu would know that she isn't going psycho on us."

"And if we can't?"

"I don't know." She shook her head. "I really don't know."

"The other option is to talk to one of the psychiatrists. I think this whole thing is a figment of her imagination," Bill said. "I really think that's what you should do."

"And the necklace? What about the necklace falling on the floor in the mornings and in the snow?" Kate asked a defensive tone in her voice.

"Has it ever occurred to you that Mary Lou could be doing that herself? Not consciously, of course, but subconsciously, to make her story seem real."

"I never thought of that," Kate whispered. "But Lulu wouldn't do that."

"Not consciously I said, but I guess the subconscious can do strange things. I've been reading a little in my spare time. Going to the library on my lunch hour and reading everything I can about the mind. It can do odd things to people. I'm out of my element here. You should really talk to one of the doctors."

Kate frowned. "I can't believe that Lulu could be doing these things herself, even subconsciously. But the music box was definitely playing when we walked into the room together."

"Kate, do you actually believe that a woman dead for forty years is trying to contact Mary Lou for some obscure reason?" Bill asked. "It's not logical."

"I know, Bill, but life's not logical. God, I feel miserable." She played with her napkin as Bill read through the notes a third time. "There's a reference here to an organization called the Friends of the Opera. I suppose I can start with that. I'll try and find out if it ever existed. If it did they might have some records of the members, at least the officers. It's really a long shot, but it's the only lead we have."

Kate looked up. "Okay, if that's the best you can do."

"Hey, give me a break. I know you were expecting me to come up with some answers but, remember, record keeping was lousy in those days. There may never have been such a group." He frowned and rubbed his chin. "Even if there was, how would Mary Lou have heard of it? She's not a historian and I'm sure she doesn't know anything about opera. Like I said, it's really a long shot, but I'll give it a try." He gave Kate an encouraging smile.

"Okay," she said, not knowing what else to say. "What'll we do now? I can't go back yet. I'm supposed to be at the movies."

"Tell you what, we'll make an honest woman out of you. Let's go see that movie. Then you won't have to ask anyone what it was all about."

"I guess. But I feel like a traitor," Kate whispered as she slid out of the booth.

Bill paid at the register. Then they walked out of the restaurant together.

Chapter 24

Mary Lou tried to pull herself together and concentrate on her paper. She read a paragraph then reread it, but it wasn't working. After about a half-hour she put the books and papers aside. I won't be able to get anything done tonight, she thought. I should have gone to the movies with Kate and the others. I don't know what to do with myself. Maybe I'll go to the chapel. Maybe I can find some answers there.

She bundled up and walked the short distance to the chapel but the windows were dark and the door was locked. Darn. Then she thought for a moment. There was a small church about three blocks down. She remembered seeing it. She decided to take a walk. If it wasn't open she would just come back; maybe stop at the little restaurant where she and Bill usually went for coffee. At least the cold air might clear her mind.

She tensed her body against the bitterly cold night and began trudging through two inches of new snow that the maintenance men hadn't gotten around to shoveling yet. She could just see the foot-prints of her classmates on their way to the theater.

Mary Lou thought of Bill. Strange, even though they hadn't seen each other in over two weeks; she realized that she didn't miss him. She kept thinking of her conversation with Jack and how much she had enjoyed being with him. She found herself comparing Bill to the charismatic doctor. Stop it, she told herself. Bill is my beau and he really cares for me. But she wasn't convinced. He said he was busy with something this weekend but she didn't remember what.

I'm getting like Margaret Montague, Mary Lou mused. Then she realized what she was thinking. Mary Louise Hammond stop this, she scolded herself. You're stepping right into your fantasy. That's sick. You're a perfectly healthy, normal young girl. In a few weeks you'll leave this place and continue with your life in the outside world. You'll leave Margaret Montague, Martha Dillard, Josephine, and all the ghosts right here where they belong.

She kept lecturing herself as she sloshed through the snow until she saw the restaurant ahead, warm and beckoning. I think I'll stop in for a minute. It's colder than I thought. As she neared the entrance she saw a young couple just leaving. There was something familiar about both of them. The boy took the girl's arm as she slipped on the pavement. She heard them both laugh.

Mary Lou gasped as she backed into the shadows of a storefront. She couldn't believe her eyes as she watched Bill and Kate walk to his car, get inside and drive away. She stood frozen to the spot, her mind a blank. Then the words came to her lips. "They're plotting against me, my best friend and Bill." She remembered Margaret Montague saying the same words in her dream. "Oh God," she said aloud and started to run.

Her legs pumped up and down, up and down. She slipped, grabbed a light post, and then continued on. She didn't know what else to do. She ran until she couldn't go any farther. She stood still, breathing hard, trying to think, but her mind was as frozen as the world around her. When she looked up she saw the church just ahead. A welcoming light shone in the rectory. Somehow her feet took her up to the door, but it was locked. Her fists pounded on the weathered wood. After what seemed like hours, a bent old man wearing a clerical collar opened the door. Tears ran down Mary Lou's face, but she couldn't speak.

"We have no service this evening," the man's voice was saying, but she didn't understand the words. She stood there, unable to utter a word.

His eyes softened and he smiled. "Won't you come in, my dear? Sit in the house of the Lord for a few moments. Perhaps you will find some consolation here."

He led her to a pew, sat her down, and settled himself nearby. Mary Lou put her head on the railing and cried out all the tears that had built up inside of her for the past months. The priest handed her some tissues. Then he sat and patiently waited alongside her.

When she finally stopped crying, her head ached, her eyes were almost swollen shut, and her nose was stuffed up.

The priest laid a fatherly hand on her shoulder. "I was just going to make myself a cup of tea. Would you like one?"

"Yes, please," she muttered. She pulled herself up from the seat and, with halting steps, followed the shuffling old man into a room behind the altar. The atmosphere of peace in this building helped her to begin to relax. Maybe I should become a nun, she said to herself. That way I would be away from the world and everything that can hurt me. But what kind of stories and nightmares might I dream up then?

When the priest returned with two cups of steaming tea, he smiled at Mary Lou and handed her a cup. "Be careful, it's hot."

She nodded and took a small sip. It was sweet and strong.

The man sat back as Mary Lou drank the tea and regained her composure. Neither said a word. When they had finished, he sat forward. "Would you like to talk about it? I am Father McDonald. I've been pastor of this church for more years than most people have lived. I've seen every kind of problem in both the young and the old. Perhaps I can help you."

Mary Lou looked at the kindly man. "I have to talk to someone, Father. If I don't, I'll go crazy." She started to cry again. The man produced a box of tissues and set it beside her.

When she had regained her composure, Mary Lou began her bizarre story. Over the next hour she told him everything, beginning with her childhood: her friend in the mirror, her mirror-image writing, her parents, Hillside, the dreams about the strange woman, and ending with the scene at the restaurant. When she told him of seeing Bill and Kate together, she was surprised that she felt more upset over Kate's betrayal than Bill's apparent unfaithfulness.

"That's quite a story," he said wrinkling his aged brow. He sat back, folded his hands and thought for a while. He hadn't expected anything like that: perhaps an unhappy love affair or an accidental pregnancy. These were the usual heartaches of young girls: not ghosts and messages from beyond the grave. He wasn't prepared for that. Perhaps this girl needed help of a different kind, someone who understood the complexities of the human mind. He had been called on to perform a few exorcisms in his long career, but he didn't think this girl was possessed. She was extremely distressed. There was a world of difference between the two.

After some thought, he decided to approach the problem from a different perspective. Perhaps she had told him the truth and the things that were happening were not a mental aberration.

He took a deep breath and reached for Mary Lou's hand. "My dear, you have been going through an extremely trying time. We of the ministry preach about the spiritual world and about heaven and hell, but we have no first hand knowledge of these mysteries, only what dogma dictates. Now, it is possible, although extremely rare, that a disturbed spirit is trying to contact you for some unknown reason. Can you accept that?"

Mary Lou looked at the man's kindly eyes. "Then you don't think I'm losing my mind?" she whispered.

"No, I do not. Suppose I do some research in the church archives and see if I can find any similar cases. I'll find out how they were handled and we can proceed from there." He hesitated for a moment then continued. "I do have a friend, a history professor, who has done some investigation into the occult. I could ask his advice. Is that agreeable with you?"

"Oh yes, yes. Those are the first positive words I've heard from anybody. Then you do believe there really was a Margaret Montague."

"Let's just say that I believe there *may* have been. Now I want you to pray regularly, to help sustain you through this experience. Here is a book of prayer. Before you go to sleep at night, read from it. And I believe that God will give you the strength to work through this trying time. Now let us pray together."

He bowed his aged head, took both of Mary Lou's hands in his, and led her through the Lord's Prayer. She felt a strength emanating from this man. She felt certain he would help her. He was the only one.

When they finished the prayer he looked into her eyes. "I want you to come back next week. Here is my phone number." He handed her a card. "Call me at any time you feel the need. As soon as I have some definite information, I'll call you. Where can I reach you?"

Mary Lou gave him the number to the nurses' residence, thanked him and left by a side door.

His parting words were, "God bless you my child."

She walked out with a lighter step until she looked around. The snow had started again, falling in huge flakes. The wind howled like an animal in distress.

"Perhaps I'd better bring the car around and drive you back," Father McDonald said as he stood by the open door.

But Mary Lou was hesitant to subject this old man to the elements for her sake. "I'll be all right," she said. "I need the exercise, to clear my head."

She bent down into the wind, wound her scarf around her nose and mouth, and began her trek back to Hillside. I should feel better, she thought as she shuffled through the accumulating snow. But I don't. She knew why. It was because of Bill and Kate. There must be a logical reason for their being together, she reasoned. But what: a surprise for my birthday? No, my birthday's in September. Scratch that. Maybe they've fallen in love with each other. The thought didn't bother her as much as it should have. She walked what seemed like miles. Then she realized she was going the wrong way. She looked up and saw the church again. She had been walking in circles.

"Easy does it, Hammond," she said aloud. "Follow the light poles. They'll lead you back to Hillside." Looking up, she calculated which direction she should walk. Then, clutching the prayer book, she began making her way back to the hospital watching the light posts as her guide.

It wasn't long before her fingers and toes lost feeling, but she continued on. "Oh God," she moaned. She was tempted to go back to the church, but realized it was getting late and the guard locked the gate at ten.

When she finally reached the iron fence, she breathed a sigh of relief. She grabbed a light pole suddenly feeling weak, as if she could walk no farther.

A figure bundled in a heavy coat and wearing a fur hat and mittens came waddling toward her. Mary Lou looked into the concerned face of Agnes, the cook.

"What you doing out in this cold little one?" the woman asked.

"I was coming from church," Mary Lou managed to answer through chattering teeth.

"Come, you warm up." Agnes took her arm and led her to the small guardhouse. She pounded on the door calling in a loud voice. "Open up." She turned to Mary Lou. "He don't hear too good." No one answered. Agnes continued to pound. "Open the door, Ralph. He's probably sleeping," she said turning to Mary Lou.

"Who's there?" a gruff voice asked.

"It's me, Agnes. Open the door you lazy lout."

The door finally squeaked open as the bleary-eyed guard looked at the two women.

"Come, come inside." Agnes literally pushed the half-frozen Mary Lou into the small shack. A space heater sat to the side issuing welcoming warmth. A half-empty bottle of whiskey and a glass stood on a table in the corner. An old radio played country western music punctuated by static.

Agnes took in the scene and frowned. "You not supposed to be drinking while you're working," she scolded.

The man frowned, rubbed his hand over two days growth of beard and whined, "Oh, Aggie, don't harp at me. It gets lonely in here."

Agnes closed the door behind them and pushed Mary Lou into a rickety chair as she looked closely at her. "Aren't you the pretty girl my Dr. Corbett brought to my kitchen?"

Mary Lou nodded, too cold and tired to speak just yet.

"Now, when you warm up, this lazy man will walk you to the Nurses' Home."

Ralph grumped, but said nothing. He simply stared at the two.

"I don't want to be any trouble," Mary Lou whispered.

"Poof," Agnes said with a wave of her arm. "He needs the exercise. Now, why you went out tonight, huh?" She scrutinized the girl with a look that said only the truth would satisfy her.

So again that night Mary Lou told her bizarre story; an abbreviated version but this time leaving out the part about seeing Bill and Kate.

"Do you believe there's a ghost roaming around here?" she finally asked looking from one to the other.

The guard frowned, squirmed in his chair, and again rubbed his hand over his chin. "I ain't seen it, but I heard it," he whispered. "A high shrill howl, like a demon from hell."

Agnes gave him a determined push. "Go on. You heard the wind. That drink can make you believe anything."

Then she turned to Mary Lou. "There's no ghost, you hear? So stop thinking those things."

But Mary Lou noticed the look that passed between Agnes and Ralph.

"I got to go home now," Agnes said. "You take this girl back nice and safe." It was not a request but a command.

The man grumbled as he got up from his chair, put on a heavy parka and took Mary Lou's arm. Neither one of them spoke as they trudged through the snow.

"Thanks," Mary Lou said as she stood at the bottom of the stairs. He merely grunted and walked away.

Mrs. Dobins stood at the door as Mary Lou practically fell inside. "What are you doing out alone on a night like this, young lady? You could have fallen in that snow and we wouldn't have found you until morning. It's happened before. Now get upstairs and out of those wet clothes and into a warm shower."

"Yes, Ma'am."

She said nothing about Agnes or Ralph as she stumbled up the stairs. When she opened the door to her room she saw Kate sleeping peacefully. Mary Lou looked at her roommate's face. She doesn't look guilty. Maybe I should wake her and confront her now. She reached out her hand, and then slowly drew it back. No, I'm too cold. I'll take a warm shower like Mrs. Dobins said. Then I'll wait 'till tomorrow and see if she says anything. There has to be a logical reason why she and Bill were together. Maybe she'll tell me on her own. Maybe....

Chapter 25

Mary Lou tossed and turned through the endless night. Every time she closed her eyes she saw Bill and Kate outside the coffee shop. Each time she envisioned the scene it became more intimate. There was no explanation that she could think of for them to be together. Maybe it wasn't them at all but two other people. Maybe she had imagined the whole thing. That thought was more terrifying than all the others. She buried her head in the pillow and cried until finally, from sheer exhaustion, she fell asleep.

In the morning Mary Lou stood at the window watching faint streaks of pink crossing the sky. She looked at the prism sitting there, its usual sparkle gone. It appeared dull and lifeless, just like her. She felt frozen to the spot as if her whole body had turned to lead. It was an effort just to move. Maybe I'll wake up and find that I've dreamed the whole thing, she thought. Maybe I'm still a little girl. She looked at her music box. Maybe I should put that away, too, she thought.

Kate was still asleep. Mary Lou wasn't sure whether she even wanted to talk to her, afraid of what she might learn. I can't just stand here waiting; I'll go crazy. What am I saying, I am crazy. She decided to take a walk. Perhaps the cold air would clear her head. She still felt chilled from the previous night but bundled up and went anyway.

As Mary Lou walked toward the door she looked again at her sleeping roommate. Then she glanced at her nightstand and at the prayer book Father McDonald had given her the night before. She walked back and picked it up. Just holding it in her hand gave her some comfort.

As she began walking around the buildings she spotted the chapel. Just the place to think things out, but, trying the door, she found it locked. Of course, it was Saturday. There would be no service until Sunday morning. She made a mental note to go. A mild breeze blew at her scarf as if pulling her in a certain direction.

Mary Lou walked on and reached the cemetery gate without consciously intending to go there. She looked at the few stones still standing. They looked sad and forlorn, long forgotten by anyone. The little white cross was barely visible beneath a blanket of snow. Mary Lou sat on a boulder and opened the prayer book. Silently she began to read.

Look unto the Lord for your solace,
Oh sinners, bow your heads.
Ask for forgiveness and it shall be granted,
Place your burdens on the altar of repentance....

Unshed tears burned her eyes. She had felt so much better after talking with Father McDonald, but now everything seemed hopeless again.

"Miss Hammond, what are you doing out here?"

Mary Lou jumped as she felt a hand grasp her shoulder. She turned to see Miss Dillard standing over her. "Uh..." she stammered, not knowing what to say.

"What is troubling you so? You seem very distracted lately," the instructor said.

"I'm not sure," Mary Lou said.

"Come in out of the cold. I want to talk to you." Martha Dillard put a protective arm around the girl and led her away from the cemetery. Mary Lou followed her instructor: yielding completely to the authoritative touch of the older woman.

The instructor opened the door to her office. Mary Lou walked into the bare room she remembered from last time. She noticed a picture of two laughing children, a boy and a girl in an ornate frame. She must have missed it before. It appeared to occupy a place of honor in the otherwise unadorned room. No pictures graced the walls, only Miss Dillard's nurse's license in a plain black frame. But on the desk sat the bud vase with a single red rose. Miss Dillard sat Mary Lou down on a hard wooden chair.

"Now, young Lady, I want you to tell me what is the matter with you. You're pale, dark circles around your eyes, easily distracted. Either you're physically ill or extremely distressed about something." She sat staring at Mary Lou waiting for an answer.

"I...I'm still having those strange dreams. I think it's this place. I'm sure I'll be all right as soon as the rotation is over." She certainly didn't want to tell her instructor everything. She might order a psych evaluation. Mary Lou feared that as much as the possibility of a ghost invading her dreams.

"I will arrange for a complete physical exam," Miss Dillard continued. "We can draw a blood profile to see if something is wrong." The woman seemed to show genuine concern.

"No, Miss Dillard, there's nothing physically wrong with me. At least I don't think so." She fought back the tears that burned her eyes.

"Many students manifest some neurotic symptoms while on this rotation. The atmosphere of a large institution such as this one can have a profound effect on a sensitive mind. Now do you want to tell me about it?" Her voice was soft and inspired confidence.

Again Mary Lou felt the catharsis of telling the story to someone who seemed to care. She told her about the dreams in more detail, finishing with her talk with Father McDonald. "I don't even know how I feel about my boyfriend anymore." She bit down on her lower lip.

Miss Dillard shook her head. "It's better not to get too involved with any one boy at your age. Finish your training. Then try different fields of nursing until you find your niche." She looked directly into Mary Lou's eyes. "Life is a banquet just waiting for you. Savor it. There'll be lots of boys. Don't let one break your heart." A deep furrow appeared between her eyes as she looked off into the distance. For a moment she seemed to be in a different world, a different time.

Mary Lou averted her eyes. She felt that she was witnessing a very private moment and felt a little uncomfortable.

Miss Dillard gave a little shake of her head and looked again at the girl. "I don't think things are as bad as you think. I don't believe in ghosts, but I've encountered some unexplainable things in my lifetime."

Mary Lou hung her head. "I have a confession to make. I think I'll feel better if I get it off my conscience. Kate Stephens and I followed you the night we met at the drugstore."

"So, it was you," Martha Dillard said, her eyes widening in anger.

"Actually it was Kate. But I'm just as guilty. We keep wondering about that little white cross. And we've seen a strange looking cat roaming around. Is it yours?"

"You may not ask anything about my personal life." The woman's face closed like a book slamming shut. "It is no one's business but mine." Martha Dillard's expression told Mary Lou that this session was over.

"My suggestion, young lady, is that you immerse yourself in something other than psychiatry. And, for the second time, I'm warning you to stay away from that cemetery." Her brows almost met in the center as she looked at Mary Lou.

"I *can* send you back to St. Benedict's School of Nursing with a request to finish your psychiatric rotation in their unit."

Her concern had suddenly become purely academic. All the warmth was gone. The instructor watched her, waiting for an answer.

Mary Lou clenched her fists. "No. Let's wait. I think the priest may be able to help me get through these last weeks. I'm sure it's all my imagination. Thank you." She got up, put on her coat and hurried out the door, running back to the main entrance to the nurses' home. She stopped for a moment and looked back to see Martha Dillard standing in her doorway--watching.

Chapter 26

Mary Lou felt a gnawing in her stomach. Was it misery or could she be hungry? She realized she hadn't eaten much in the past twenty-four hours. *I wonder what time it is? Are they still serving breakfast?* As she ran toward the dining room she looked at her watch. There was still time. She stopped in the doorway. Kate sat at their table playing with her fork. She seemed absorbed in thought. She sipped coffee and stared at the half-eaten roll on her plate. Mary Lou decided to act as if nothing had happened.

"Hi Kate," she said.

"Lulu, where have you been? I looked all over but couldn't find you." Relief flooded Kate's face.

Mary Lou shrugged. "I couldn't sleep, so I went for a walk."

"Where?"

"Around. No place in particular." She waved her hand in the air. "But I did work up an appetite. Where's our waitress?"

"She's not here today. We have someone new. She wants everyone to work on her case."

"What do you mean?"

"You'll find out. Here she comes now."

A short, chubby, middle-aged woman bounced up to the table. Straight salt and pepper hair, cut in a Dutch boy cut, framed a round face giving it a youthful look. Bright red lipstick smeared from one end of her generous mouth to the other. Two circles of rouge adorned her prominent cheekbones. It gave her the illusion of a pathetic clown.

"Hello," she whispered close to Mary Lou's ear. "I'm new here, but I won't be staying long. My name is Rosie and I want you to work on my case. Please get me out of here. There's been a conspiracy. I'm a famous Russian actress kidnapped from my home in Siberia. They put me in here so I couldn't perform before the

Czar. It's very important that I return home as soon as possible." She began to dance around the table humming a folk tune.

"Rosie," Kate called her back to the present. "Please get my friend some break-fast. She's hungry."

Mary Lou looked at her. Am I really your friend, she wondered?

"Yes, yes. Right away," Rosie said. "Good rolls this morning. Very good rolls."

"She's kind of pitiful," Mary Lou said with a sigh as the woman hurried away.

"Yeah, real delusions of grandeur," Kate said.

A strained silence hung in the air. Mary Lou waited for Kate to say something, but she simply sat there, staring at the half-eaten roll on her plate. Rosie returned in a few moments setting a feast in front of Mary Lou: juice, boiled eggs, bacon and flaky rolls.

"My goodness, Rosie," Mary Lou said. "This is a breakfast fit for a queen."

"Yes," the woman whispered looking around her. "You are the Queen. You won't forget to work on my case now, will you?"

"I'll try, I really will." She watched the woman dance away and whisper in the ear of another student.

Poor pitiful soul, Mary Lou thought. She'll probably spend the rest of her days telling the same story to every new student who comes here.

She turned her attention to Kate. "What's the matter?" she asked, a cutting edge to her voice. "Something on your mind? It's not like you to leave food on your plate."

"I'm not hungry this morning. I guess I don't feel very well. I think something disagreed with me."

It's guilt, Mary Lou thought.

"If you don't mind, I'm going back to the room and lie down. I feel kind of nauseous." Kate picked up her coat and hat and stumbled out of the dining room.

A few moments later Blanche and Carol came in. They waved and took their assigned seats. Blanche mumbled something to Carol glancing at Mary Lou.

She finished her breakfast in silence, then decided to test the two. She walked over to their table. "Hi, how was the movie last night?"

"It was great. Humphrey Bogart and Lauren Bacall in *Key Largo*. You should see it."

"Did Kate enjoy it?" she asked noticing their discomfort.

"Umm, I guess so. Did you ask her?" Blanche responded.

"No. She doesn't feel well this morning, went back to the room to lie down." She noticed the two exchanging glances.

"Did you eat something after the movie?" Mary Lou persisted.

"No, no goodies. We came right home. It was starting to snow again."

Mary Lou grimaced. "Blanche, I know Kate wasn't with you last night. Where was she and why?" Mary Lou towered over the girl glaring at her.

"I don't know, honest. Ask Kate, not me." She squirmed in her seat.

"Okay, if that's the way you want to be, but don't ask to borrow my notes for the exam. No go, unless you tell me the truth. I won't give them to you, and that's a promise." She held her ground. I'll get the truth out of these two yet, she thought.

"Gee Mary Lou, don't be that way. They're planning a surprise party for you. Kate and Bill. Don't spoil it."

"A surprise party? Whatever for?"

"I don't know. That's what Kate said. Now I told you. I betrayed a confidence. I hope you're satisfied." She sat back with her arms folded across her chest like a pouting child.

"Sorry Blanche, I didn't mean to do that, but there was something I had to know. Mum's the word. About the party I mean. I won't tell Kate about our conversation. Bye."

Mary Lou walked out of the dining room thinking. I don't believe a word of that. What a dumb excuse, surprise party. And these two believed it. Not too bright. I'll let Kate stew another day. Then I'll confront her, tomorrow.

For some reason she felt better. Her step was lighter and her mind clearer. She realized that she hadn't had a dream in three nights.

That was positive. But she knew that Margaret Montague wasn't finished with her. I won't let that woman keep me in this place, she promised herself. I'll find her and put her to rest.

By suppertime, Mary Lou had finished the first draft of her research paper. She had spent most of the day in the library while Kate stayed in bed. She was so absorbed in her work that she didn't notice Dr. Corbett until he sat down next to her.

"Hi," he said.

"Oh, Dr. Corbett, I mean—Jack." She found herself blushing and willed it to stop.

"What are you working on so diligently?" he asked, his handsome face wreathed in a smile.

"I'm finishing my research paper," she said blowing out a sigh of relief. "I think that's the end until the final exam." She sat back in the chair and returned his smile.

"You look better than the last time I saw you."

"I am feeling much better." For a moment she wanted to tell him about her dreams and about Margaret Montague, but she hesitated. I think I can handle it, she thought. I don't need a psychiatrist, yet.

"Agnes told me she found you out in the cold last night." He frowned and rubbed his chin. "Be careful. Hypothermia can set in pretty quickly." His boyish look almost made Mary Lou smile.

"I will. Promise."

"Well, I'll be off," he said. "If you need to talk to me, my office is in building five."

"Thanks." She sat there for a long time after he left unable to sort out her feelings. Then she pulled her mind back to the task at hand. All she had to do now was give the paper one more edit and type it. Bill's sister had promised to do that for her. Bill—he was supposed to be visiting relatives this weekend. Why all the lies and deception? Why couldn't he just tell her the truth? If he had stopped caring for her, she would rather know. Maybe her bizarre behavior made him reconsider. He might not want her for his life partner. What a mess.

She picked up her papers and returned to the nurses' home to find Kate talking on the phone.

"Yes, Mom. I've been eating like a pig. Have to lose a few pounds. All my clothes are getting tight...."

Mary Lou passed without acknowledging her. She walked into their room and threw herself on the bed. She was so tired. She stretched lazily and, tucking her right hand under the pillow, touched something metallic. As she pulled it out, the silver chain lay in her hand, like an omen.

When Kate came into the room, Mary Lou was holding the chain in her hand, looking at her accusingly.

"Did you do this? Is it some kind of sick joke?"

"What? Did I do what?" Kate ran over to the bed.

"My chain. The one you supposedly locked in your jewelry box. It's here under my pillow. Only you had the key."

Kate sat on the bed and stared at the chain. "I didn't put it there, honest. You have to believe me. The last time I saw it was when I locked it up, just like you asked."

Kate went to her dresser and took the key out of the vase. She unlocked the jewelry box and looked inside. The chain was gone.

A sick suspicion ran through Mary Lou's mind. Suppose Kate wanted to help her over the edge to get Bill for herself. Suppose she had deliberately put the chain under the pillow. No, this is my best friend. Then she remembered her dream. Margaret Montague's best friend had betrayed her. She decided to confront Kate, here and now.

"All right, I want the truth. You're a terrible liar. What's going on between you and Bill?" Mary Lou sat up straight and looked directly into Kate's eyes.

"Nothing, what makes you think that?" Kate paced from one end of the room to the other.

"Stop lying!" Mary Lou shouted. "You were together last night. I saw you."

Kate stared at her friend for a moment then burst into tears. "Oh, we were just trying to help. We were worried about you so we decided to meet and talk about it. When did you see us?"

"I couldn't concentrate so I took a walk. I saw you two come out of the restaurant laughing. Then you got into Bill's car."

Kate blurted out the whole story relieved to get it off her chest. "I'm so sorry we deceived you. We didn't know what to do to help you." Kate sat on the bed with tears streaming down her face.

"I guess I have been acting loony lately. You both think I'm a mental case and didn't want to tell me."

"I'm scared," Kate said. "And Bill doesn't know what to think." She looked so miserable that Mary Lou gave her a hug.

"But Bill is going to search for some trace of this woman in old newspaper archives and for this society, Friends of the Opera. You do understand, don't you?"

"I suppose." She blew out a long breath. "I have to prove to Bill and to myself that this is all real and not just in my mind. He won't want competition from a ghost. But the chain under the pillow—if you didn't put it there and I didn't either, who did? And what about the music box playing without being wound by either one of us? Don't those things prove something?"

"It sure seems like it." Kate's voice mirrored her fear.

The girls stared at each other for a long time. A chill permeated the room; the lights overhead flickered ever so slightly. The radio had been playing soft music. Now they heard a low piercing strain. The announcer's eerie voice commanded their attention.

"Welcome to *Inner Sanctum*. Tonight's episode, *Cause of Death*, is guaranteed to keep you in———suspense...."

Kate quickly turned off the radio. "Come on, let's get out of here. We're both getting edgy. It must be time for supper."

Chapter 27

That night Mary Lou removed all writing materials from her bedside table. She was not going to make it so easy for Margaret Montague to leave any more messages. She tossed and turned for a long time until she climbed out of bed, sighed, and walked to the window looking out at the clear, cold night.

A few more weeks and I'll leave this place, she thought. Will I ever be the same again? Will Margaret Montague ever leave me alone?

Mary Lou thought of her life before coming to Hillside. It had been so orderly, so predictable, so comfortable. Now it was chaos.

She wondered if Bill still felt the same about her. Then she thought about her feelings for him. Did she want to spend the rest of her life with him? She remembered Miss Dillard's words: "Life is a banquet. Savor it." They kept repeating over and over in her mind.

Finally she yawned and crawled back into bed, but her dreams were not of her future: but of something else.

Margaret Montague lying in bed...the same room...trying to kill me...my husband and my best friend plotting...stealing... locked in this room....

Mary Lou saw everything clearly: the sick woman, the threatening husband, and the locked door. When she woke, she was more concerned about Margaret Montague than she was disturbed by the dream. That evil man really was trying to kill her. She quickly grabbed the notebook and wrote down the dream. Then she sat back and read all the notes from the beginning. The story seemed to be reaching a climax. Hmm, I wonder how she got to Hillside? A wealthy woman like that certainly wouldn't be hospitalized in a state facility Mary Lou rationalized. Well, I'm sure she'll tell me. She's been directing the show all along.

"Lulu, are you sure you'll be all right? I can phone my aunt and tell her I can't make it, or you can come with me. Why don't you?" Kate pleaded.

"No, I'm fine. Go to your aunt's house and have a good time. The kids will be waiting for you. I'll see you later. I've decided to go to church this morning."

"Church? Since when did you get religious?"

"Since Friday." Mary Lou showed Kate the prayer book and told her all about Father McDonald.

"It's all my fault," Kate moaned. "If I hadn't lied to you...."

"Don't be silly. You did what you thought was best. Besides the good Father just might be able to help me. I'm going to call him tomorrow night."

The church service was comforting: prayers, hymns, and the traditional sermon. At one point the sun put in a brief appearance through a small stained glass window throwing a rainbow of colors across the altar. Mary Lou took it as a good omen. She read from her prayer book: something she would cherish all her life. She saw Miss Dillard sitting in the next pew, but the two barely exchanged glances.

After the service Mary Lou realized she had the entire day to herself. She walked around outside for a while considered looking up some of her classmates to see what they were doing, and then decided not to.

A head covered with a thick wool cap popped out from behind one of the buildings. Josephine's scrawny body followed, bundled in an oversized coat. Mary Lou stifled a grin at the sight of her. Josephine beckoned her with a mitten-covered hand. At first Mary Lou ignored her, but Josephine kept waving. I'd better find out what's on her disjointed mind, she thought. She walked toward the woman who was now bouncing up and down.

"I know a secret," she said giggling, "about Martha and Ben."

Mary Lou's eyes widened. "Tell me, what's the secret?"

"Chocolate. Give me chocolate, then I'll tell."

"Okay." Mary Lou let out a sigh. "But I have to go back to my room and get it. Will you wait for me?"

"At the cemetery," Josephine said and sprinted off.

This is a waste of time, she thought. But I have nothing better to do right now. She hurried to her room, retrieved two chocolate bars that had escaped Kate's eagle eye, and went out toward the cemetery.

True to her word Josephine was waiting there, dancing around and singing a hymn.

"Josephine," Mary Lou called. "Here's your chocolate." She held out one bar keeping the other in her pocket.

The woman grabbed it, pulled off the wrapper and shoved it in her mouth, finishing it in three bites. "Mmmm, good. More." She looked at Mary Lou expectantly.

"Oh no. You promised to tell me the secret."

Josephine grinned, making silly faces. She sidled up to Mary Lou and whispered in her ear. "Martha and Ben—doing naughty things in the storeroom. I saw them touching and kissing and doing naughty things." She danced around again cackling her characteristic laugh.

Oh my God, Mary Lou thought. They were lovers. "So what's buried in that grave with the little white cross?"

Josephine greedily held out her hand. Reluctantly Mary Lou gave her the other chocolate bar. She wolfed it down as quickly as the first.

"Well?" Mary Lou waited.

"I saw her. Little tiny." She held out her hands about six inches apart. "Little tiny box. Buried it in the cemetery. Puts flowers on it all the time."

"Who buried it, Josephine? Was it Miss Dillard?"

Josephine nodded vigorously. "Martha and Ben, Martha and Ben—doing naughty things. Josephine knows. Josephine knows everything." With those words she ran off jumping over mounds of snow and singing.

When Kate returned Mary Lou could hardly wait to tell her what had happened. Kate stood there, her mouth open, unable to say a word. "Wow, that's quite a scandal. Do you think it's true?"

Mary Lou shrugged. "Who knows? Maybe Josephine made up the whole thing."

"Just a minute," Kate said picking up her notebook. "I did have time to write down a few things before old Dill Pickle grabbed that chart out of my hands." She thumbed through the pages until she found what she was looking for.

"Here, it says Dr. Ben Turner was admitted in nineteen thirty five at age thirty-seven." She did some elementary math in her head. "That would make him fifty-two now. Do you think that's about right?"

"Sounds right and he looks about that age. So, what do you think?" Mary Lou looked at her roommate as if expecting some words of wisdom to come out of her mouth.

"How old do you think Dillard is?" Kate asked.

"Gee, who knows? She could be anywhere between forty and fifty I guess." She shrugged. "That sounds right, too."

"Yeah," Kate said. "Suppose old Dillard was working here then and she and Ben Turner had an affair and she got pregnant." She looked at Mary Lou, her eyes wide with excitement.

"Josephine said the box was only about six inches long. Suppose she lost the baby and buried it in the cemetery. That would explain the little cross and the flowers." Suddenly Mary Lou felt an overwhelming sadness. She looked at the stern Miss Dillard in a different light. "I feel kind of sorry for her."

"Me, too," Kate said. "We better not say anything to the others."

"No, definitely not. We have no right. Leave her with her heartache and her secret." Mary Lou plopped on the bed and sighed. "Well, if it's true, that's one mystery apparently solved." No wonder she told me to savor life, Mary Lou thought, not to concentrate on one boy. Maybe that's what she did and now she's trapped here in sort of a time warp.

"Did you ask Josephine about the ghost?" Kate asked breaking into her thoughts.

"When I heard what she said I forgot all about the ghost. Besides, I didn't have any candy bars left."

"Well then, we'll just have to buy some more."

Chapter 28

The following day Mary Lou went to the drugstore after lunch to buy more chocolate bars. This is going to use all my spending money if I'm not careful, she thought. Then she went to find Josephine.

She looked everywhere and was just about to give up when the woman popped up in front of the nurses' residence.

"Chocolate. I want more chocolate," she demanded, dancing around and giggling.

Mary Lou held out one of the bars in front of her. "First tell me about the ghost."

"Ha, ha, the ghost," Josephine danced and cackled. "The ghost was a lady, a very rich lady."

"How did she get here and what does she want?" Mary Lou persisted.

"Don't know," Josephine mumbled. "Don't know what she wants. But I saw her. I saw her lots of times. Yes, I did." She nodded vigorously and reached for the candy bar, but Mary Lou held it back.

"Not yet. Tell me more. What does she look like?"

Josephine opened her eyes wide and looked around as if expecting to see the specter. "White," she said. "White and filmy, like a mist. Dark hair flowing down her back and black eyes that look right through you." She jumped at the bar, but Mary Lou held tight.

"Just a minute. I think you're making all this up. I don't think you know anything at all about the ghost. I don't think there is a ghost."

Josephine looked nervously from side to side, and then crept up close to Mary Lou blowing her fetid breath in the girl's face. Mary Lou stepped back trying to keep from grimacing.

"She's here." Josephine said. "She wants something. She told me so."

"What does she want, Josephine? What?"

"She wants to be free...free like me." She grabbed the candy bar, tore off the paper, scarfed it down, and then stood there, waiting.

Mary Lou thought for a minute and then pulled the other bar out of her pocket. She watched the woman eye it greedily.

"Not yet. What about that animal that roams around? It looks like a big cat."

Josephine's eyes widened. "It's a ghost cat," she whispered. "When it howls something bad is going to happen." She held her hand out for another bar.

Mary Lou frowned and shook her head. I don't believe that, she thought. "One more thing. Do you know where the old records are kept? I mean the very old ones?"

Josephine nodded. "I know...I know everything." She grabbed for the bar, but Mary Lou put her hand behind her back.

"Show me first, then I'll give you this candy."

The wiry woman sprinted off through the snow with Mary Lou close behind. Where in the world is she going? Probably on a wild goose chase.

Josephine ran behind a number of buildings then toward one of the many small brick structures that dotted the complex.

She stopped and pointed. "In there."

"How can I get in?"

Josephine laughed and ran to the back. An ancient door with a rusted padlock hung at a strange angle. The woman pointed, grabbed the candy bar and ran off, dancing and singing.

Mary Lou looked at the lock. It might be easy to break into, she mused. But now I'd better get to class before I'm late. I'll tell Kate and, maybe we can come back here tonight.

"Are you actually thinking of breaking into that record storage shed?" Kate asked looking at her friend in amazement. "I didn't know you had it in you. My roommate, the burglar." She looked at Mary Lou and laughed.

"It isn't funny. If I can find any trace at all of this Margaret Montague, maybe I can figure out a way to be free of her. Josephine said that's what she wants, to be free."

"And you believe Josephine?"

"I don't know." She threw herself on the bed and lay there, staring at the ceiling.

"Okay, Lulu. We'll give it a try after supper. Have you got a flashlight?" Kate asked.

"I think so." Mary Lou searched through her drawers and came up with a sturdy one. "My mother gave it to me in case the power goes out."

"Score one for your mom." Kate said.

As soon as they finished dinner, the girls took a small screwdriver that Kate had in her drawer, the flashlight, a pad of paper and pencil and made their way to the record building.

"Maybe we should do this in the daylight." Mary Lou looked around to make sure no one was watching them.

"We're here now," Kate said. "Besides, in the daylight someone's liable to see us. Here, shine that light on this old padlock. Let's see if I can pick it with this screwdriver."

Mary Lou held the flashlight with a shaking hand as Kate bent over the rusty lock. She watched as her friend twisted and turned the tool trying to engage the bolt.

"This isn't working," Kate said. "There's got to be another way." She looked around. "Up there, see? Is that a little window?"

Mary Lou shone the light up above the door and to the right. "It sure looks like one, but it's awfully small."

"Help me move this rock. Maybe one of us can climb through."

"I don't think so," Mary Lou said as she helped her friend roll a large rock underneath the window. "There, now what?"

"I'll climb on the rock and see if I can reach the window," Kate said.

"Be careful."

Kate reached her arm up and, grabbing the bottom of the sill, tried to push the window open. After a futile attempt, she gave up. "No good. Let's get back to the padlock." Again she tried to open it with the screwdriver, but it wouldn't budge.

"This isn't working," Mary Lou said, disappointment reflected in her voice. "We need a key."

"I guess it's back to Josephine," Kate said. "We'd better go out and buy more chocolate bars."

The next day Kate cornered Josephine in the hallway leading to the day room. "Look what I've got," she said holding out a bar.

Josephine grabbed for it, but Kate said, "Not so fast. We need the key to that record storage building and I'll bet you know where it is."

Josephine's eyes widened. Then a cunning smile crossed her face. "Maybe I do, but I need two bars for that."

"It's a deal. Give me the key and I'll give you both of these bars. They're full of raisins."

When Kate returned to the room, she was humming a tune.

"What are you hiding?" Mary Lou asked. "I can tell by the look on your face."

Kate held out a key: an old one of unknown vintage.

"Where did you get it?" Mary Lou asked. "Josephine?"

"Uh huh. As soon as it starts getting dark we'll go back and see if it works."

Chapter 29

Soon after they finished their duties on the wards, they left the nurses' residence armed with the flashlight and the notebook and pencil. The sun was just beginning to sink behind a bank of clouds.

"There's still enough light to see that lock," Kate said. "Let's go."

Mary Lou was beginning to have misgivings about this venture. What if they got caught? What would the consequences be? Worst of all was the possibility that they would find nothing. But it might be her only chance to prove that Margaret Montague had been a real living person.

When they reached the building, they looked around to make sure no one saw them. By then it was dusk; the light was waning fast.

"Okay, shine that light on here while I try this key," Kate said. "Who knows, it might not even be the right one."

They looked at the rusted old padlock, then at the key and stared at each other.

"What a couple of klutzes we are," Kate moaned. "This isn't a padlock key. That sneak Josephine must have picked it up somewhere just to con us out of chocolate bars."

"Now what?" Mary Lou asked.

Kate shrugged. "I guess we give up."

"No!" Mary Lou shouted. She looked around and spied a sturdy rock. Picking it up she gave the padlock a resounding whack.

"What are you doing?" Kate asked looking at her roommate in amazement.

"I haven't come this far"—whack——"without trying"—whack—"everything." To her surprise the padlock fell apart with the last whack.

They looked at each other. "I guess we're officially guilty of breaking and entering," Kate said with a smirk. "Come on, let's push this door open."

They leaned against the old door as it slowly swung inward. The eerie creaking sound raised the hairs on the back of Mary Lou's neck. It seemed to say, "You don't belong here."

"Shine the light around," Kate said. "See if there's some kind of a switch or something."

The beam of the flashlight roamed over rows of old file cabinets stacked up to the low ceiling. "There's a dirty bulb hanging down," Mary Lou said. She reached up and pulled the chain; a weak light filled the room with an unearthly glow casting weird shadows in every corner. "I can't believe it works," she said glancing nervously around.

"Yuck, there's spider webs all over the place," Kate said rubbing webbing off her face. "I hate to think what else there might be in here."

"This place is creepy. We'd better hurry before somebody finds us," Mary Lou said.

"Now just who do you think is going to find us?" Kate asked. "From the looks of this place nobody ever comes here."

They looked down at their footprints in a thick layer of dust that appeared undisturbed for many years.

"Okay, where do we start?" Kate asked.

"You start at one end of the cabinets and I'll take the other," Mary Lou said. "We're looking for dates around 1911 or earlier."

They began pulling open squeaking drawers that seemed to resist the intrusion. There wasn't any system at all; just records and papers stuffed inside. Some drawers were jammed and the girls spent time prying them open. Most of the papers they found dated from the twenties and thirties. After about an hour they looked at each other and shook their heads, wiping dust off their faces and sneezing.

"This is hopeless," Kate said. "Why don't we come back another time?"

"I'm not ready to give up yet," Mary Lou said. "Look, there's something back there—in that corner." She sneaked behind a cabinet and was greeted by a fat spider in a web directly in her path.

"Oh God, a spider." She cringed as it darted away. I invaded your territory, she thought. So I guess I can't blame you.

"Kate, here's a cabinet that looks much older than the others." With some difficulty she pulled out a rusty drawer. The papers inside were yellow with age: some typed, some hand written in the flowing spidery penmanship of years gone by. "Look, these are really old."

Kate ran up to her and stared over her shoulder. "What's the date?"

"Poor Farm established in 1851," Mary Lou read. "Wow, look at this. The building was three stories high, built of brick, costing twenty-five thousand dollars. In 1858 the insane asylum was completed by the Dunstun trust. Overcrowding was a problem." She read on. "A hundred and sixty acre farm worked by inmates. Here's a copy of the Warden's Annual report of the Insane Asylum and Poor House. The date is December 30, 1876."

Kate grabbed some papers and began to read. "Look, thirty babies were born in the Poor House. That's pretty sad. This is interesting, but it's not getting us the information we're looking for." She picked up another report and began laughing.

"Here's a list of the causes of insanity. Listen to this: fright, fatigue and excitement, intemperance, jealousy, excessive mental application, masturbation. If that was really true every man would be psychotic, and a lot of women, too."

"Oh Kate, you're impossible. Look, here's a picture of the day room in male ward sixteen showing overcrowding. Those poor sad-looking people. Here's another one of the women's ward."

Suddenly she froze. Her hands began shaking. "Kate, look at this picture. That woman looks like Margaret Montague: the one in the old fashioned wheelchair, there, at the side of the picture, see? She's slumped over, but you can still see her face."

Kate looked at the picture and shook her head. "Lulu, I know how anxious your are to find this woman, but this picture is so old and faded that you can't recognize anybody."

"I'm taking this with me. Maybe there's some way to enlarge it. What was that sound?"

Kate grabbed her arm. "I don't know. I think someone or something is in here."

They stood frozen to the spot. A furry animal streaked across the floor.

"Oh God, what was that?" Kate whispered.

Mary Lou was too frightened to answer. Suddenly the light began to flicker; then went out. Mary Lou felt something brush against her legs. "Ugh."

Kate snapped on the flashlight and directed it at two yellow eyes staring at them. Just as quickly, the animal ran out. They heard an unearthly yowl from outside.

"I'm out'a here," Kate said.

Mary Lou grabbed the folder she had been searching and followed her friend. She almost forgot to close the door, but forced herself to turn around and pull it shut.

They looked around, but saw nothing. Still, a foreboding feeling filled them both as they ran back to the nurses' home.

Chapter 30

That night Mary Lou opened the folder and read through the record. She found the names of physicians in charge at the turn of the century. The chapel was built in 1936, the hydrotherapy building in 1939.

The pictures that the documents painted were bleak: overcrowding, the number of indigents living there, and families crammed in because they had no place else to go. But there were also a few pictures of the farm in 1908: chickens and vegetables grown by the inmates.

"What are you reading there?" Kate asked coming in from talking with the other girls.

"These pages from the record room are really interesting, and sad, too. Did you know why this place is sometimes called Dunston?"

"Didn't Miss Dillard say it was named after some man?"

"Wealthy Andrew Dunston set up a trust when his daughter was declared insane. He wanted this to be the most modern facility of its day."

"Yeah, what else?" Kate picked up a yellowed sheet and squinted at the almost illegible writing.

"Listen to this. Here's a list of the inmates by occupation: actors, bakers, butchers, broom makers..." she went down the list... "homemakers, horseshoers, physicians."

"Oh?" Kate raised her eyebrows. "Any nurses in the bunch?"

"Nope, don't see any listed," Mary Lou said.

"Put that stuff away for now," Kate said. "We don't need to know all that."

"I guess you're right." Mary Lou put the papers back in the folder but kept out the picture of the women's ward. She stared at it long and hard. Is that you, Margaret? Is it? Are you trying to tell me you were a real person?

When Mary Lou climbed into bed, her head was swimming with all the things she had read. She tossed and turned for a long time before she fell into a restless sleep.

Terrible medicine...trying to kill me....so tired...getting dark...he's turning on the gas lights...not lighting them...smell the gas...can't stay awake...can't breathe....

When she woke, Mary Lou was gasping for breath. "another dream, Kate."

"Ugh?" Kate mumbled, rubbing her eyes.

"Another dream."

"Okay, tell me and I'll write it down."

"I could see him turning on the gas jets but not lighting them. He was so cruel looking. He wanted to kill her."

Kate looked at her roommate with real concern. "All right, I've got it all down here. Try to forget it now."

"Forget it? How can I forget it? This has been plaguing me since we got here. I'd better call Father McDonald tonight. I have to see him again."

Mary Lou stood in line impatiently waiting for her turn to make a call. When the line was finally free, she grabbed the phone and looked at the paper in her hand. With trembling finger she dialed the number.

After five rings the soft voice of the minister answered. "Rectory, may I help you? Father McDonald speaking."

"Father, this is Mary Lou Hammond. Remember me?"

"Indeed I do, my dear. I've been praying for you. How are you feeling?"

"Much better, thank you. I was wondering if you have any information for me." She bounced from one foot to the other.

He hesitated for just a moment. "I had a long talk with my friend the other day. He had some rather interesting things to say. In fact, he would like to meet with you. Can you come to the rectory on Wednesday evening?"

"Yes, I can," she answered eagerly. "What time shall I be there?"

"Will seven-thirty be agreeable with you?" he asked.

"That's fine. I'll see you then and thank you so much. Good bye."

"What did he say?" Kate asked when Mary Lou came bouncing into the room.

"I'm going to see him on Wednesday. His friend wants to see me, too. He didn't say any more than that, but by the tone of his voice I got the feeling he believes me. Oh, I hope they can help me." She clasped her hands and sighed.

Kate looked at her friend and bit down on her lip. "Then I'd better give you these. They might mean something." She produced the two messages that she had taken from the floor. "I'm sorry. You were so upset that when I found them, I was afraid to give them to you. I did show them to Bill though. We decided it was better if you didn't see them just then."

Mary Lou's face set in a frown. "Kate, I know you mean well, but please stop interfering. Let me be the judge of what's best and what's not." There was a cutting edge to her tone.

Kate looked down at the floor. "I'm sorry."

"Just forget it." Mary Lou immediately regretted being so brusque with her friend. She knew she was just trying to help. She walked over and gave her a hug. Kate smiled and hugged her back. "When is Bill supposed to call? I want to talk to him."

"I was supposed to call him about eight. It's almost that time now."

The girls went out into the hall but had to wait for the phone. Mary Lou twisted her fingers nervously. She hadn't talked to Bill in four days. Strange, she didn't miss him at all.

When the phone was finally free, Kate grabbed it and dialed the number. "Hello Bill, it's Kate. Everything is okay here, but I have to tell you something important. I told Lulu about our conversation. I couldn't help it. She saw us."

Mary Lou watched the changing expressions on her friend's face and could just imagine Bill's reaction.

"Yeah," Kate continued. "She went for a walk and saw us coming out of the restaurant. She's right here. Hang on." She handed the phone to Mary Lou and went back toward their room.

"Hello, Bill."

"Hi," Bill answered. "It wasn't a good idea, was it?"

"No," Mary Lou answered, an edge to her voice. "I'm not a child. I don't appreciate being lied to."

"Okay, don't get your hackles up. Let me make it up to you. Why don't I come up there now? We'll go for a cup of coffee and talk about it."

"But it's eight o'clock already." Mary Lou was still bristling.

"I can be there in a half-hour. The door isn't locked until ten, right?"

"Yeah."

"Okay, that gives us an hour and a half. And bring me your paper so my sister can type it for you. I'll see you soon."

"Mary Lou stood with the phone in her hand, her brow furrowed. What would she say to Bill? Should she show him the picture? She hurried back to the room and began picking through her clothes.

"What are you doing?" Kate asked.

"Changing. Bill's coming over and taking me out for coffee."

"Did he find out anything? In the archives I mean—in the old newspapers?"

Mary Lou looked surprised. "I didn't even ask. We'll talk about it when I see him. I have to give him my paper for his sister to type."

Kate moaned. "Gosh, you're finished with yours already and I haven't even put my notes together."

"Well, you'd better get to it. Nobody's going to do it for you," Mary Lou said. "Why do you always leave everything until the last minute?"

"You're right. I'll start tonight." Kate sat at the desk and began sorting through scraps of paper and pages of notes.

"Good luck," Mary Lou said as she buttoned her wool sweater, grabbed the folder with her paper, the envelope with the picture, her jacket, hat and gloves, and ran out the door.

Mary Lou alternately peered out the windows and paced the floor. Mrs. Dobins kept frowning at her.

As soon as she saw the car drive up, Mary Lou hurried out. Bill jumped out to open the car door for her. Then he slid into the driver's seat and gave her a peck on the cheek.

She inched away, suddenly not wanting his attention.

Bill shrugged, started the car and drove off the grounds. They talked about everyday things: classes, family, the weather, but not the ghost—not yet. They remained on neutral ground as long as possible.

When they were comfortably seated in the restaurant, coffee and pie in front of each of them, it was time.

"Tell me the truth, Bill," Mary Lou said, anticipation in her voice. "Did you find any trace of Margaret Montague?" She almost didn't want to hear the answer.

"Do you really want to know?" he said.

She nodded.

"I couldn't find any record of a woman by that name. But, I found something about that organization, Friends of the Opera. The organization did exist and there were a few names, but nothing even close."

Mary Lou played with her coffee cup and let out a sigh of disappointment.

Bill's expression brightened. "I did find one name that interested me. You said her friend was called Agnes Calumet, didn't you?"

Mary Lou nodded, her eyes pleading for something positive.

"There was a reference to the last president of the organization in 1906 named Agnes Calem. It could be a misprint. It's really a long shot and I know it doesn't help you one bit." He gave her a commiserating look.

She sighed. "Thanks for taking up your time on a wild goose chase like this. I knew it was hopeless. Did you check the newspapers?"

"Yep, I did, as much as I had time for. I'll go back again tomorrow, but it's like searching for a needle in a haystack, looking through all the obituary notices for the year 1911."

He sat back in the booth and shook his head.

"It is a needle in a haystack, but she's real. I know she is."

She thought for a moment: then decided to tell him about Father McDonald. "I went to see a priest."

He looked at her with a question in his eyes. "A priest, why?"

Briefly she told him the story and the planned meeting for Wednesday.

"Maybe I should go with you," he said.

"You don't have to. I'll be all right."

"I want to hear what he has to say." A determined look crossed his handsome face.

Mary Lou wasn't sure if she wanted him there. "Okay," she said finally. "Pick me up at seven. But it's really not necessary." Why was he so eager to go along? Did he think he might find out something she wouldn't otherwise tell him? Oh there I go, she thought, suspicious of everyone.

"What are you holding in your hand?" he asked.

"It's probably nothing, but...." She told him about the search through the old records, and then held out the picture.

"You two could have gotten into a lot of trouble breaking in like that."

"I know, but I was desperate."

"What's this supposed to be?" he asked looking down at the grainy picture.

"I found it in one of the file cabinets. This sounds silly I know, but that woman in the wheelchair looks like Margaret Montague."

Bill studied the picture then raised his eyebrows. "There's no way you can identify anyone from this picture. It's old, faded, dark, and the faces are small. You're imagination is taking over I'm afraid."

"Isn't there some way that part of the picture can be blown up, just that one face?"

Bill shook his head. "It's not that simple. It would have to be re-photographed and then enlarged. By that time it'll lose any contrast that's there. I don't think it'll work."

"Couldn't we try?" She pleaded, clinging to the only lead she had.

His look softened. Then a smile crossed his face. "Sure, why not. I'll take it to school tomorrow. My pal, Jim, is working evenings in the photo lab. I'll see if he can do anything with it. But don't get your hopes up. This one is more than a long shot."

Chapter 31

Mary Lou watched anxiously as winter raged over the next twenty-four hours. Twelve inches of heavy wet flakes fell, paralyzing all forms of transportation. People were left stranded; power lines fell under the weight of the snow and the onslaught of the wind. Winter held the city in its tight grip and refused to let go.

Despite the hissing radiators, the wards never lost their chill. Patients huddled in corners. The nurses' home was no better. Everyone wore sweaters and jackets but never felt warm.

Mary Lou looked out the window wondering how she would get to see Father McDonald tonight. His friend surely won't be there. We'll have to postpone the meeting. What a mess. I want to tell him about my most recent dream, how real it seemed. Did Margaret die from the gas? She couldn't have. She had to get to Hillside. Oh, everything is so mixed up. I just want it to be over. She stood at the window willing the snow to stop.

Around noon it did; the sun shone, and, as the city began digging out, Mary Lou's spirits rose. She decided to phone Father as soon as she got off duty. She could see garbage trucks fitted with snowplows chugging along the road. By evening the streets should be passable. She breathed a sigh of relief. Maybe tonight she would get some answers.

"Are you still going to go out tonight?" Kate asked. Her look said, forget it.

"I'm going to call right now. The streets are pretty clear so I don't see any reason why I shouldn't be able to go."

She went to the phone and stood in line waiting impatiently until her turn came. Her trembling fingers dialed the number. "Hello, Father McDonald, this is Mary Lou Hammond. I was wondering if your friend would be able to make it tonight. The weather's been pretty bad."

"Yes indeed, my dear. He has just arrived. We're going to have dinner together and share a few memories. Shall we expect you at seven-thirty?"

"I'll be there. And, is it all right if my boyfriend comes along? He's anxious to meet you."

"Of course. He's more than welcome."

No sooner had she hung up than the phone rang.

She picked it up. "Nurses' residence."

"Mary Lou, is that you?" Bill's strained voice asked.

"Hi, Bill. I just talked to Father McDonald. His friend is there and everything's all set for tonight. I thought the weather might change the plans, but it seems to be okay right now."

"I've got a real problem. I'm at school and the snowplow buried my car along with a half a dozen others. It's a mess. The way it looks, we might not be able to dig out until tomorrow so I'm going to have to take the bus home. I really wish you wouldn't go tonight."

"Oh I'll be fine. All the streets are clear around here. Even some of the sidewalks are shoveled. My two feet will get me there. I'm really anxious to hear what this man has to say. Listen, there's a line forming behind me. I'll call you tomorrow. Bye." For some reason she was relieved that Bill wasn't going with her. Why: because this was just between her and Margaret Montague?

In the early evening heavy gray clouds covered the sun. A light snow began falling. Mary Lou and Kate listened to the radio. The weatherman predicted another major storm for the Chicago area.

"You'd better not go, Lulu," Kate cautioned. "They say another three or four inches, blowing and drifting. Stay here, please." She turned pleading eyes to her friend.

"I'm going and that's final. Don't worry. It's only a six-block walk. See I'm bundled up just like I'm going to the North Pole."

"I'm going to worry until you get back," Kate said. "Are you sure I can't go with you?"

Mary Lou shook her head. "Thanks, but this is something I have to do alone. Look out the window. The main streets are clear," she said, even though they were not visible from their window. The world looked cold, bleak and forbidding. The wind whistled through the ill-fitting window frame. It was a penetrating cold: a Chicago cold.

"Besides, the church is only a half block off the main road. No problem." She sounded braver than she felt. I'd better take my prayer book with me, she thought. I might need it.

"Put that scarf around your mouth and nose to warm the air you breathe," Kate said.

"Yes, Mother Kate." Mary Lou laughed nervously. "I'm only going six blocks. Don't worry." She bounded out of the room with a feigned confidence. Am I being foolish? She wondered. Is this a waste of time besides being dangerous? But she was determined. If she didn't do everything in her power to free Margaret Montague, she would never be free herself.

From the window Kate watched Mary Lou trudging through the drifting snow with her head down, protecting her face from the biting wind. Kate silently said a prayer.

"Phone for Mary Lou," a voice called from the hallway.

"She's not here," Kate answered. "I'll take it."

She went to the phone and picked up the instrument. "Hello, this is Kate. Mary Lou isn't here right now."

"Kate, it's Bill. Has she left already?"

"Yeah, I was just watching her from the window slugging her way through the snow."

"Oh no. There's another violent snowstorm coming this way. I was calling to tell her not to go."

"She was dressed for the Arctic, said it was only six blocks and she would be fine. I tried to talk her out of it, but she wouldn't listen. She said she had to do this."

"She's so stubborn," he said, an exasperated tone to his voice. "Do you have that Father McDonald's phone number?"

"No, I don't."

174 Helen Macie Osterman

"Well what's the name of the church? I'll look up the number."

"Gosh, I don't know that either. She never mentioned it. Maybe I should go after her," Kate said with some misgivings.

"No, don't do that. Just tell her to call me as soon as she gets back."

"I will. Bye." The phone was heavy in her hand when she placed it back on the receiver. There must have been something I could have done to prevent her from leaving. If anything happens to her I'll never forgive myself, she thought. It's all because of that damned ghost. I wish we had never come to this place. Kate shuffled back to her room, picked up a book and tried to read, but all she could think of was her friend trudging slowly through the snow, the wind whipping around her, and the cold biting her hands and face.

This is worse than I imagined, Mary Lou thought. How far have I gone? It seems like miles. I wish that wind would let up. Those blasts are icy cold even through all these clothes. I'll walk a little faster; maybe that will help. She picked up her pace, but the wind blew against her as if determined to drive her back.

Up ahead she saw the restaurant. Maybe she would stop for a cup of coffee and a warm up. But when she looked at the darkened store and the closed sign, she shook her head. I guess they didn't expect customers on a night like this.

After what seemed like hours she spotted the rectory, just visible through the falling snow. It was coming down now in huge flakes and swirling in the unrelenting wind. Mary Lou promised herself not to stay too long. She didn't even want to think of the trip back.

Father McDonald welcomed her into the vestibule. "I really didn't think you would come out on a night like this. I was about to call you and tell you to stay at Hillside. Come in and have some hot tea."

He ushered the shivering girl into the warm rectory. She took off her coat and hat, shoved her mittens in a pocket, and slipped out of her boots then sat down to a hot cup of tea and raspberry scones.

"This is my friend, Doctor Miller. He's a psychologist," he said smiling down at her.

She saw a much younger man looking something like the photographs of psychiatrists that hung on the wall at Hillside. He probably thinks I'm a nut case for coming out on a night like this, she thought. "My roommate tried to talk me out of coming, but this is too important to me. I might not have another chance to meet you, Doctor Miller. Someone has to help me solve this dilemma if I'm ever going to have a normal life again." She took a sip of the hot liquid. It was strong and sweet, like the first time.

"I admire your determination, Miss Hammond," he said. "Now if you have thawed sufficiently, suppose you tell me your story. Sit back and start from the beginning."

Mary Lou nestled into the deep cushion of the armchair enjoying the warmth of the room. She began to talk and continued non-stop for the next hour. She showed the two men the mirror-image messages and the notebook of dreams. When she finished, she felt drained and exhausted. She let out a deep sigh and bit into a scone.

"That's quite an experience," Doctor Miller said as he exchanged glances with his friend. He nodded and tented his fingers under his chin. "I have seen a few similar cases in the past. You see I've studied parapsychology for many years. It's a fascinating subject. There's so much we have yet to discover. Of course neither science nor the church accept any of this, not yet, but someday they'll have to. I do believe that research into the paranormal will be accepted in the not too distant future." He smiled at her, finished his cup of tea, put it aside and folded his hands on his knees.

"Let me tell you what is happening here. When a person dies, the spirit, soul, astral body, whatever you choose to call it, leaves its physical counterpart and goes to another dimension. That's what clergymen refer to as heaven or hell. It's a complex concept dealing with the coarseness of matter, but, simply put, the spirit leaves the body and departs for greener pastures." He smiled again. "Am I making sense?"

"Yes, please go on." Mary Lou sat forward in her chair, fascinated by all this. She had never heard anything like it before.

"Sometimes a spirit becomes what we refer to as earthbound. That simply means it has left the physical body, but is unable to find its way to the other realms. It's more common in cases of violent death, such as murder or accidents. This Margaret Montague sounds like a very strong-willed spirit. She seems to want to exonerate herself. She mentioned revenge, another reason to cling to the physical world. Now this spirit is trapped, unable to interact with the physical realm because it has no body, yet unable to find its way to the next dimension. So it stays in a sort of limbo hovering close to the physical remains. Do you understand?" His keen eyes looked at Mary Lou.

She bit down on her lower lip and thought for a moment. "It does make sense, in a strange sort of way. But why was she able to contact me? What can I do to help her be free?"

He shook his head. "I can't answer that. Perhaps there is something in your spiritual makeup that facilitated that contact. At any rate, it happened. As I said, this seems to be a very determined spirit. Now she wants your help."

"How do I do that?" Mary Lou asked feeling helpless and more frustrated with every passing moment.

"That can be a problem. Some people work with mediums and psychics. What you can do is try to communicate with the spirit through your mirror-image writing. That seems to be her contact with you. Write messages to her telling her to release her hold on this physical plane, to let go of her anger and resentment. Those feelings are holding her here. Tell her to let go, to depart for the higher planes, to the next life. Tell her you believe in her. That seems to be very important to earthbound spirits. Be compassionate, but be firm. Tell her that even though you understand her dilemma, you refuse to be used by her any longer. That approach should work."

"I'll try anything. I want to be free as much as she does." Mary Lou was filled with a sense of purpose. At least now she had a plan.

"Now my dear," the priest interrupted, "the snow is complicating your young life. I suggest you leave immediately while you can still see the street or you may have to spend the night here."

Mary Lou looked up. "Oh, I couldn't do that." She had lost all track of time. The hands of the clock pointed almost to nine. When she looked out the window, she saw an alien white world with snow swirling ominously.

"The automobile is in the shop or I would offer to drive you home," the kindly man said.

"I'll be all right. It's safer on foot than in a car in this kind of weather anyway. You would just get stuck in a snowdrift. What I really need is a pair of snowshoes." She tried to laugh off her nervousness. She thanked the two men, bundled herself up, and started back.

When she walked out the door the wild slapped her like a fist. Wow, she thought, this is a real blizzard. A person could get confused and lost in something like this and freeze to death even a few feet from shelter. She had read stories like that. She remembered the last time she was at the church and it started to snow. She had gone in the wrong direction and it wasn't nearly as bad as this. I've got to be careful.

She decided to walk in the street and use the streetlights as guides. There certainly were no cars out, so the street was her best bet. Huge mounds of snow lined the curbs where the plows had piled it earlier. She felt as though she were walking through a canyon with mountains of snow on either side. In some places the drifts were taller than she was. She was completely isolated and alone.

She had to keep her bearings as she slowly moved from one streetlight to the next. An eerie sound reached her ears. What was it: someone in trouble, an animal? She shook her head. Just the wind. But the sound crawled under her garments with more terror than the wind. It was unearthly.

She decided to pray. She tightened her scarf around her nose and mouth and began reciting the 23rd Psalm:

"The Lord is my shepherd,
"I shall not want,
"He maketh me to lie down...."

She couldn't remember the words. The swirling snow clouded her mind as well as her vision. Real terror gripped her. The snow kept swirling in a blinding blanket; the wind kept howling like a snarling animal. She realized she was not only afraid but also angry.

"Margaret Montague, this is all your fault. You got me into this mess and I'm doing my best to help you. Right now I could use a little help from you."

Talking to the unseen ghost gave her some comfort. She plodded on, head down, unable to see, moving by rote from one lamppost to the next. When she tried to move her face she thought the skin might crack open. I'm freezing. Keep moving. Keep moving, she told her self over and over.

After what seemed like hours she saw the intersection. The gate should be just ahead. She breathed a sigh of relief. But what if it were locked? What would she do then? She couldn't find the side-walk so she would have to estimate. She finally managed to reach the fence. Another sigh of relief. At least she had gotten this far. She couldn't feel her fingers and toes anymore and her face was a tight mask, but she was almost there. Now I'll just hang onto this fence until I find the gate, she thought. Ralph should be at the gatehouse and I can warm up. He'll probably help me back to the nurses' home.

She clung to the fence for her very life. This was her only contact with this savage environment. Step by halting step she finally reached the gate. To her relief it stood open, lodged ajar by piles of snow.

"Thank God," she almost shouted. The gatehouse should be right over there, she thought as she staggered along. Suddenly she bumped into the darkened structure. When she found the door locked, she pounded on it, willing it to open. "Ralph, let me in, please." No response. She turned the knob back and forth hoping it might open, but nothing happened. He was gone. There was no way she could get inside.

Mary Lou looked around wildly, searching for some landmark. She had no idea which way to go. She had lost all sense of direction. The sound of the wind seemed to be warning her of her dangerous predicament.

"Damn you, Margaret Montague. You hateful bitch! This is all your fault. If I freeze to death out here there will be nobody to help you!" She shouted her frustration into the wind.

Slowly the snow in front of her began to swirl in a counter-clockwise pattern, different from the main body of the blizzard. It turned and twisted gracefully, assuming a vague human shape. Then the mass began to move away from the gatehouse.

Mary Lou stood, mesmerized. Was she imagining this? Could it really be the ghost leading her to safety? She had no other choice but to follow the illusion, stumbling, falling, and then picking herself up and plodding on as the mass continued to move. She continued on as if she were in a trance. As suddenly as it had taken shape the mass dissolved. Mary Lou looked around. A dim light shone directly in front of her. She reached for the banister with unfeeling hands and pulled herself up the stairs to the nurses' home: tears streaming down her half-frozen face. She almost fell into the entryway.

"Miss Hammond," cried Mrs. Dobins. "Miss Hammond is safe. Where have you been, child? Everyone has been worried to distraction." The stern matron threw a blanket around the shivering girl and led her to a chair.

"Even Miss Dillard is here," she said.

Mary Lou's body shook uncontrollably. She couldn't speak; just sat there, glad to be alive. She looked up into Martha Dillard's stern gaze.

"Miss Hammond, do you realize you could have frozen to death out there? The radio is broadcasting disaster bulletins warning everyone to stay indoors. We are responsible for your safety. I'll speak with you later about your conduct." Her voice sounded stern, but reflected real concern. She turned to the matron. "Get some hot chocolate into this young lady, Mrs. Dobins." She looked down at Mary Lou with an almost caring expression.

Kate burst into the room. "Lulu, Lulu. My God, you're all right." She hugged Mary Lou and cried, repeating her name over and over. "Bill has called every half-hour," she said.

"Kate, call and tell him I'm okay. I'm too shaky to talk to him right now." Her hands trembled so badly she could hardly hold the cup of chocolate Mrs. Dobins handed her.

"How did you find your way through that awful blizzard?" Kate asked.

Mary Lou took a swallow of chocolate and smiled. "I had a guide," she whispered in Kate's ear. "Margaret Montague."

I owe you my life, Margaret, she thought. Now I'll help you find yours.

Chapter 32

After she thawed out, Mary Lou told Kate everything that happened. "Wow," Kate said, her eyes bulging, her mouth agape. "What are you going to do now?"

"Well, I think I'll start tonight by writing a backwards message to Margaret. I'll put it on my nightstand with the silver chain on top of it, since that seems to be some sort of a link with her. That's all I can think of. I hope this works. Then she and I will both be free. We only have a little over a week."

Mary Lou couldn't stop shaking even though she wore flannel pajamas and heavy socks and snuggled under three blankets. "I'm so cold and so tired. I feel as though I'll never be warm again."

"Miss Dillard said you should see Dr. Corbett," Kate said, a silly grin on her face.

Mary Lou didn't answer, just crept further under the blankets searching for warmth she couldn't find.

Kate walked over and hugged her protectively. "It's all going to be okay. This is almost over. I'm here and Bill's standing by. Even old Dill Pickle is on your side. With all this backup, you'll make it."

Mary Lou smiled. "Thanks, you're a good friend. I'll tell you one thing. I'll never forget these three months as long as I live. Now I'd better start writing. Hand me a piece of paper and a pencil, please." With reluctance she pulled her arms out from under the covers.

Kate walked over and got the supplies from the desk.

"Oh, and my prayer book, too. I'll need that. I think I'll start every message with a prayer."

She thumbed through the book, but everything seemed too stiff and formal. Then she closed the book, put her right hand on top of it, took the pencil in her left hand and began to write.

Look not into the darkness but into the light.
Release all feelings of hatred and revenge.
They are binding you to this earth plane.
Let go and be free.

The pencil slipped out of Mary Lou's hand as she began to doze. Kate looked at the note, nodded, put it on the nightstand and turned out the light. Then, remembering her friend's plan, she took the silver chain out of her jewelry box, tiptoed back to the bed and placed it on top of the note. She tucked the blanket around Mary Lou's pale drawn face and climbed into her own bed.

Mary Lou settled down as the dream came.

Margaret hearing voices through a fog..."asphyxiation...brain damage...never be the same again...private home in Lake Forest...."

In the morning Mary Lou found the note and the chain on her nightstand. "I don't remember putting them there." She looked at Kate, a question in her eyes.

"I did," Kate said. "You fell asleep and I remembered what you said."

"Thanks. I don't know if it did any good. Nothing seems to be moved, but we're dealing with a spirit here." She realized how strange those words sounded, even to her. "I hope she read it. And I had another dream. Write it down please."

"I don't blame that lady for hating her husband," Kate said as she wrote the dream in the notebook. "He was a real no good. I wonder what ever happened to him?"

"I don't want to know," Mary Lou answered. "It's bad enough knowing about Margaret. He probably ran off with her best friend and spent all of his wife's money. That seems to be what they were planning. Oh well, I'm sure Margaret will tell me." Mary Lou felt a chill and pulled the bathrobe tighter around her. "It's funny, Kate, but I feel that it's all coming to some sort of climax. I would still like to know how she got here to Hillside."

"If she really did," Kate said. "We haven't found any proof that she was here. In fact, if you want to be realistic about this whole thing, there's no real proof that this woman ever existed."

Mary Lou shook her head. "Oh she did. She's real. Some things you know without proof and this is one of them. I wonder if Bill's friend was able to do anything with that picture."

"Speaking of Billy Boy, he's coming over tonight," Kate said.

"Why didn't you tell me?"

"There was so much commotion last night that I forgot. You told me to call him and tell him you were all right. When I did, he insisted on seeing you. He also said he had something to give you."

"What time is he coming?" Mary Lou felt conflicting emotions. Did she want to see Bill now? What would she say to him? And what did he have to tell her? Was it something about the picture?

"He said about seven-thirty. Has to dig his car out first."

"Okay." Mary Lou slumped back down in bed and cuddled under the covers. Her throat felt scratchy; her head ached; her nose was stuffy. Darn, she thought, I've caught a cold traipsing around in all that snow. I'll be lucky if I don't get pneumonia. She decided to drink an extra glass of orange juice for breakfast and go to bed early. She dragged herself out of bed, washed and dressed, and put a cardigan over her uniform, but still felt a shaking chill.

When she looked out the window at the barren landscape, she saw drifts of snow four feet high. The caretakers looked like automatons outside. First dig the shovels deep, lift, pile to the side, and then start again, keeping time as if orchestrated by an inner rhythm. Paths began to emerge between the buildings of this isolated world. That's exactly what it is, she thought: an isolated world, bound by the wrought iron fence and cut off from everything normal. These people have no conception of time, joy or happiness. They exist in a vacuum: sleeping, waking, and living from one meal to the next, waiting for the next dose of medication. This is a prison worse than death. And Margaret Montague's trapped here. No wonder she wants to get out. "I have to set her free," Mary Lou mumbled.

"What did you say?" Kate asked.

"Nothing. I was just thinking out loud. It still looks pretty nasty out there." She shivered as she drew way from the drafty window.

"It's about five below according to the radio," Kate said as she too, put a sweater over her uniform. "They said it's supposed to reach ten above later today, a real heat wave." Kate listened to the news religiously every morning. It was one way of keeping in touch with the outside world.

"Do you have any throat lozenges?" Mary Lou asked. "I feel a little hoarse and scratchy this morning."

"I wonder why," Kate said: a note of sarcasm in her voice as she looked in her dresser drawer. "Here are some, lemon flavored and fortified with vitamin C."

Mary Lou eagerly took the box and put one in her mouth. She grimaced. "They don't taste very good, but if they do the trick, it's worth it."

"Come on, Lulu, let's go to breakfast. I'm starving."

After breakfast when they entered the classroom, Mary Lou met Miss Dillard's scrutinizing gaze.

"I want you to report to the infirmary before you go on the wards," she instructed.

"Yes, Ma'am." Mary Lou really didn't see the necessity, but she knew better than to contradict Miss Dillard. Besides, they might be able to give her something besides those awful cough drops.

With her scarf wound tightly around her face, Mary Lou walked along the cleared sidewalks toward the infirmary. Something half-buried in the snow caught her eye. She bent over to look then drew back in disgust. A freshly killed half-eaten rodent laid there, blood still oozing from the dismembered limbs. Then she saw a vague shape dash around a building.

She shivered as she ran into the warm infirmary. The place almost looked like a regular hospital: clean white tiled walls, spotless linoleum on the floor. She looked around for a nurse or receptionist, but saw no one.

"Hello," she called.

"Be right with you," a cheery voice answered.

Mary Lou sat in one of the straight hard-backed chairs lining the walls. A radiator hissed in one corner.

Soon a short rotund woman bustled in wearing a traditional white uniform with a nondescript nurse's cap on her head. Her face wore a welcoming smile. "You must be the student Miss Dillard called about."

"Yes, but I feel okay, really," Mary Lou said.

"We'll just check you out." She led Mary Lou into an examining room and pointed to the table. Mary Lou took off her coat and hat and climbed up.

The nurse took her vital signs and wrote them in a record.

The door opened and Dr. Corbett walked into the room. He raised his eyebrows and smiled. "We meet again, Mary."

"Everything is normal," the nurse said.

"Good. Just let me listen to your chest and look at your throat and you'll be out of here. Lie back and relax."

After a thorough examination, he said, "Your chest is clear, but your throat looks pretty red. As long as your temperature remains normal, we'll just treat it as a mild upper respiratory infection."

"I'm okay, really," she said listening to her hollow words.

He sat down beside her and bit the side of his cheek. "Now what was so important that sent you out into a blizzard?"

Mary Lou sighed. "I guess I'm just like Don Quixote fighting windmills."

He frowned. "Unless you have a Sancho Panza to keep an eye on you, I suggest you stay indoors, understand?"

"Yes sir."

He opened a cabinet and handed her a bottle of cough syrup. "This should relieve some of the soreness."

"Thanks," she said gratefully taking the bottle.

"Don't make me worry about you, Mary. I have enough to keep me occupied with this place. And just remember that you'll soon be out of here and will be leaving all these memories behind."

She nodded as she left the infirmary. But will I, she thought. Will I ever be free of Margaret Montague?

Chapter 33

"Miss Hammond," came the matron's grating voice. "You have a visitor."

"Thank you, Mrs. Dobins. I'll be down in a minute." Mary Lou looked at her reflection in the mirror. She saw a pale drawn face with dark rings around her eyes. Even her curly hair seemed to have lost some of its sheen. She hastily ran a comb through it. I need some makeup, she thought. She rifled through Kate's makeup kit, knowing her roommate wouldn't mind. A little cover up under the eyes, some rouge on the cheeks, a hint of lipstick. That was much better.

Now add a little bounce to your step, she told herself as she left the room. Don't let Bill know how lousy you really feel. She put her palm to her aching forehead. I don't think I have a fever, just a mild sore throat. I'll be fine in a few days. She reached into her pocket and found another lozenge, popped it into her mouth, buttoned her sweater and hurried down the stairs.

She saw Bill pacing nervously in the reception parlor. He took both of her arms in his hands and scrutinized her face. "Are you okay?" he asked, a worried look on his face.

"I'm fine, Bill, fine," she lied.

She saw the way he looked at her. The makeup doesn't fool him. He knows I'm not well.

"Hmm." Mrs. Dobins stood in the doorway, her arms folded across her generous bosom.

Bill smiled at her and let go of Mary Lou. "I promise we're just going to sit here and talk for a while." He flashed her one of his enchanting smiles.

The woman turned way, frowning. She stayed in the next room where they knew she could watch them.

"I'm not going to stay long," Bill said. "I just wanted to see for myself that you're all right and give you this." He handed her a folder. "My sister finished typing your paper. I know you'll have to hand it in soon, so I thought I'd bring it."

"Thanks," she said, swallowing the sandpaper feel of her throat. "And thank your sister for me. I don't know what I would have done without her help."

He pushed her curls away from her face. "You look tired; you need all the rest you can get. Pretty soon I'll be taking you out of here." He held her hand, and then touched her cheek. "Do you have a fever? You feel kind of warm. Did a doctor see you?" His tone was anxious.

"All I need is rest. I did see one of the doctors. He said to come back if I get worse. I've got cough syrup and these awful tasting cough drops, see?" She pulled the box out of her pocket. "Anything that tastes this bad has got to make me better." She tried to laugh, but suddenly all she wanted to do was lie down.

"Kate said you had something to show me." She looked at the envelope he held in his hand, the same one she had given him. "Was your friend able to do anything with that picture?" she asked almost afraid to hear the answer.

He shook his head. "He suggested using a magnifying glass. Here, I brought you one." Bill held the powerful magnifier over the face on the picture.

Margaret Montague's face popped out at Mary Lou. It was blurred and her head hung to the side, but it was definitely the woman in her dreams. "It's her, I'm sure of it. That's the woman I've been dreaming about. Oh Bill, don't you see, this proves that she existed, that she was here." Mary Lou felt tears prickling behind her eyes.

"Sure it does," Bill said with some doubt in his voice.

Mary Lou looked at him. "You still don't believe me. I can see it in your face. But I know it's her, and I'm going to prove it." Her lower lip trembled as she fought back the tears, tears of frustration and exhaustion.

"I'll try to help all I can. Go to bed now. Tomorrow I'm going to follow a few more leads in the newspaper archives."

Mary Lou knew he wasn't telling her the truth. There were no leads. He was just humoring her. She knew he didn't believe her, probably thought she was delusional. Maybe she was. "Thanks, I appreciate it." She heaved a deep sigh. "I am tired. All I want is to go to bed."

She went with him to the door. He gave her a peck on the cheek under the watchful eye of Mrs. Dobins.

Mary Lou turned toward the stairway. It seemed steeper as she climbed one step after the other. Her legs felt like lead. God, I can hardly make it, she thought. For a moment she froze. Was that an image before her eyes, something in the corner, something filmy? She grabbed the railing to keep from falling, squeezed her eyes shut then slowly opened them. Spots danced before her eyes. She sat down on a step and lowered her head until the wooziness passed, then gripped the rail and pulled herself up the stairs. I need sleep, that's all, sleep. Her throat felt as if it were lined with a heavy grade of sandpaper. What a time to get sick. There's so much to do. At least Bill brought my paper. I'll hand it in tomorrow. And exams are next week. I'll have to study. I'm so glad I don't have to stay in this place much longer, she thought as she reached her room.

She could hear laughter down the hall. She knew Kate and some of the others were planning to study together. They sounded as though they were having a good time. I wish I could join them, she thought. But she was so tired. Have to write a letter to Margaret Montague. She closed her eyes for a moment then took the pencil in her left hand and began to write.

Dear Margaret,
I found your picture.
I know how miserable you were here in this place.
Let go of that life that was so cruel to you and gave you so much pain.
Let go of Samuel and Agnes.
Go on to a better life.
    Your friend,
    Mary Louise Hammond

She stood the picture against the lamp on the nightstand, put the note next to it and placed the silver chain of top. "Can't keep my eyes open any longer." She flopped into bed, fell asleep almost immediately, and began to dream.

    In this institution...getting a little bit clearer in my head...what are they saying? No more money? Samuel is gone? Everything is gone? Transfer to the Hillside Insane Asylum....

"Wake up, Lulu. Didn't you hear the alarm? Hey, what is this? A shrine?" Kate looked at the picture propped against the lamp, and the note with the chain lying on top. "Come on, we'll be late for breakfast."

Mary Lou groaned. "Just let me lay here and die. I feel awful."

"Aren't you going to tell me about the picture?" Kate asked.

"It's Margaret Montague, that's who it is. Bill brought me a magnifying glass. It's her and last night she told me how she got here." Mary Lou sneezed then fell back in bed. "Oh my head, my nose, my throat."

"Okay, tell me about the dream and I'll write it down." Kate sat on the side of the bed and wrote down Mary Lou's words. Then she looked closely at her. "You do look awful. Do you have a fever?" She placed her hand on her friend's forehead. "You feel kind of hot to me."

"It's just a head cold and sore throat. That's what Dr. Corbett said. I'll be all right. I'll keep sucking those lozenges and taking that cough syrup and I'll survive the day."

"You could stay in bed, you know. Dill Pickle would let you."

"I know, but we have that review for the exam next week. Right now I need all the help I can get. Besides, I have to turn in my paper. Bill brought it last night." She looked up at Kate and tried to smile. "Come on, give me some inspiration. How many more days?"

Kate smiled. "Seven more working days and we're free." She danced around the room making clowning faces.

Mary Lou smiled and tried to feel some of her friend's enthusiasm. She forced herself out of bed and plodded down the hall to the bathroom. Only seven more days...seven more days...seven....

Chapter 34

Mary Lou struggled through the day thinking, "if I'm not better by to-morrow...." She attended the review class, but was too sick to benefit from the two-hour session. She alternately shivered with chills and sweat with fever.

Miss Dillard took her aside after the class. "I don't like the way you look, young lady. I'm taking you back to the infirmary right now."

Mary Lou looked at the instructor feeling too miserable to protest. She nodded, put on her coat, hat and mittens, and, on rubbery legs, followed Miss Dillard out the door.

The bright sunshine belied the sub-zero temperature. At least the wind had died down and the cold momentarily revived her. She listened to the sound of their feet crunching on the frozen snow as step-by-step they neared the infirmary. More than once Miss Dillard turned and grabbed Mary Lou when she lost her footing.

When they reached the building, Mary Lou felt as though she could barely move. Miss Dillard ushered her into the warm examining room, had her take off her outerwear and lie down on the table.

Mary Lou closed her eyes and dozed for just a minute but was awakened by a wracking cough. She looked up into the frowning face of Jack Corbett. He held a thermometer in his hand.

"Under the tongue," he said. He took her hand and felt her pulse. Mary Lou could feel a pounding at her temples. She knew her heart was beating much too fast.

When he took the thermometer out of her mouth, he looked at the reading and shook his head. "One hundred and one. And your pulse is racing."

He did a thorough examination, looking at her throat, listening to her heart and lungs, feeling her lymph glands—all under the watchful eye of Miss Dillard. Then he sat down and looked into Mary Lou's anxious face.

"Right now I think all you have is a severe upper respiratory infection. Your lungs are clear and your throat is inflamed, but I don't think it's anything more serious than that. My prescription is bed rest, lots of fluids, and, definitely chicken soup." He smiled. "Don't ask for a medical reason, because there isn't any. But the old grand-mothers' remedy is still the best. And I'll give you something for that cough."

He turned to Miss Dillard. "I'll see that this young lady gets back to the nurses' home. Now I'd like to speak to her alone for a few minutes." He gave her an engaging but dismissive smile.

He turned to Mary Lou, sat back in his chair, and folded his hands. "Now, Mary, I want you to tell me what this is all about and never mind Don Quixote. No one goes out in the kind of weather we had the other night without a good reason. What is it? A boy-friend?" He raised his eyebrows and pursed his lips.

The girl slowly turned her head from side to side. "You're not going to believe me," she whispered.

"Try me."

In halting tones, between bouts of coughing and sips of water, she told him her story. She looked at his expressionless face. "You think I'm delusional, don't you?" She almost didn't want to hear his answer.

"I don't think that at all. There's definitely something going on. I agree, to a certain extent, with the clergyman that there are many things we don't know. As for a spirit from beyond the grave...." He left the sentence unfinished.

"What's wrong with me?" she asked in a pleading tone.

"I think you need to get out of this place. You're extremely sensitive and impressionable. As soon as you leave next week, this will all pass."

"You really think so?"

"I know it. Now let me get a bottle of a stronger cough syrup and don't go out under any circumstances until I clear you. Understand?" His look gave no room for discussion.

She nodded then began another bout of coughing.

When Bill called that evening she was in bed, as ordered.

"Lulu, Bill's on the phone," Kate said. "What shall I tell him? You're too sick?"

"I'll talk to him, otherwise he'll worry." She pulled herself out of bed, put on her bathrobe and fuzzy slippers and padded down the hall to the phone.

"I'm feeling much better, honest," she lied when he voiced his concern. "I saw the doctor again. He said I had a cold and sore throat; gave me a stronger cough medicine and it seems to be working. I'll be okay in a day or two."

"Well you don't sound like it. Are you sure there's nothing else?" He hesitated for a moment. "Promise me you'll stay in bed and follow orders."

"I will."

"All right." That answer seemed to satisfy him. "I'll call you again tomorrow night."

"And, Bill, did you find anything else in the archives of the newspapers?" She already knew the answer to that.

"No, I'm sorry—nothing."

She dragged herself back to the room and crawled in bed. She didn't have the strength to eat anything although she did force down the chicken soup. She thought briefly of Jack. He was so considerate. No, I can't start fantasizing about him now. I have to concentrate on getting well and getting out of here.

The wastebasket overflowed with used tissues; the skin of her nose and upper lip were red and sore from blowing and wiping. The cough syrup did control the hacking a little, but her irritated throat remained raw.

The temperature outside continued to drop. A north wind howled finding every crevice in the ancient window frame. Mary Lou shivered with another chill. I don't think Hell is hot, she mused. I think it's cold, cold as Chicago in winter.

Kate opened the door quietly, munching on a doughnut. "How's it going?" she asked looking at her roommate and the barely touched tray. "Did you drink the chicken soup?"

"Yeah, but I feel like hell," Mary Lou whispered. "Ah—choo! Do'd get too close. I do'd wa'd to sdeeze ad you. By throat is like coarse saad paper."

Kate thought for a moment. "You know when I was a kid my grandmother used a lot of folk medicine. One thing she did really helped. At least I think it did. She took a washcloth, soaked it in cold water, and wrapped it around our throats. It was chilly at first. Then she wrapped a piece of flannel around the cold cloth."

"Like hydrotherapy, huh?"

"Yeah, just like the cold wet sheet packs. The cold makes your body send more blood to the throat and helps it to heal. They didn't have much else back then."

"Led's try id." Yes.

Kate went to the bathroom and came back with a thin washcloth that she had soaked in cold water. She wrapped it around the front of Mary Lou's neck. "We don't have any flannel. What can we use?"

"Scarf." Mary Lou pointed to her woolen scarf lying on the chair.

Kate wrapped it loosely around her throat leaving the fringed end lying across the pillow. "There, how does that feel?"

"Okay."

"Try and get some sleep. I'm going to Blanche's room for a little while, but I'll check in every few minutes to see if you're all right."

"Thags, Kate." I should write a note to Margaret Montague, Mary Lou thought, but I'm too sick tonight. I'll do it tomorrow. I hope she doesn't mind. She looked over at the nightstand. The note from the previous night still lay there alongside the picture and the silver chain. In a few minutes the washcloth became warm and cozy. It felt good. She fell into a deep sleep.

196 Helen Macie Osterman

People screaming and crying...in a hellhole...can't move right arm...can't walk...sit in chair all day...crazy person waving her arms...running...yelling...hands around my throat...squeezing...can't breathe...help....

The dream was so real. Mary Lou could feel the tightness around her throat, compressing her windpipe. She couldn't take a breath. She thrashed around reaching for something. At that moment Kate opened the door, turned on the light and ran to her.

"Lulu," she cried pulling the scarf from around her neck. The fringe, caught on a corner of the bare bedspring, pulled tight as Mary Lou struggled.

Mary Lou gulped in breaths of air. "Oh my God. Id was awful. Couldn't breathe. Dream."

"Here have a drink of water." Kate's shaking hand held the glass to her lips. "It's okay, you're all right now. That scarf was a dumb idea. I should have known it could be dangerous."

"I'b aw right," Mary Lou said. Her head throbbed; her throat was so sore she could hardly swallow; her body burned with fever. "Kate have to write dowd the dream"

"All right," Kate said with a heavy sigh. "Here's the notebook and pencil. Write it down. But, for heavens sake, don't talk. I can't understand you any-way."

She watched Mary Lou scribble the dream on the paper; then lay the pencil and a sheet of paper on the nightstand. Kate propped her up on two pillows, tucked the extra blanket around her, put a fresh glass of water next to her, and turned out the light.

It was still early so Kate decided to read for a while. She turned on a small lamp on her nightstand and picked up the notebook. She felt a chill as she read the last entry. The scarf was strangling Mary Lou at the same time she dreamed about Margaret Montague's death. How weird, Kate thought. I'll be so glad to see her out of this place. But would this be the end of the dreams? What did this Margaret expect Lulu to do? Kate glanced at her sleeping friend.

What if she had more than a cold; what if it turned into pneumonia. I'd better watch her, carefully.

Chapter 35

The morning dawned cold and overcast. The wind continued to howl through the old building. When Mary Lou got up to go to the bathroom, she realized she had slept all night without a dream. She felt weak, but better. She hoped she had dreamed the last of Margaret Montague. The story was over, but something was unfinished. What was it? The woman wasn't free yet. Mary Lou could sense it. *I didn't write her a note last night. I'd better do it this morning.*

"How are you today?" Kate asked.

"On the mend. At least my nose isn't so stuffy. My throat's still raw and I'm coughing, but I think my fever is gone."

"Good. You stay in bed. I'll tell Mrs. Dobins you're still sick and you need at least another day in bed." Kate looked up at the ceiling and bit her lower lip. "I'll tell Dill Pickle that you're feeling better but not ready to come back to class yet. Maybe she'll send that cute Dr. Corbett to see you again. Hmm, maybe I don't feel so good either."

Mary Lou smiled at the look of relief on her friend's face. She did feel better, but the deep, hacking cough remained despite the sugary syrup.

"Now get back in bed and stay there. No fancy tricks or I'll put you in restraints. You're definitely not leaving this room today." Kate peered out the window. "Look at those clouds. It's going to snow again. And listen to that wind. Brrr." She folded her arms around herself and moved away from the window.

"Here are some magazines and the notes for the exam. I'll turn on the radio to your favorite station. And here's another pillow so you can read." She adjusted it under her friend's head. "And, a glass of water. You have to push fluids you know."

"Oh Kate, you're such a good nurse." Mary Lou managed a smile. "Give me some more of those lozenges, too." She began coughing. "I'll be fine," she said when the paroxysm stopped.

Kate frowned. "I'm going to find Dill Pickle right now and give her an update. And remember, don't leave this room."

"I won't. I promise." There's no way I could make it any farther than the bathroom, even if I wanted to, she thought as she watched Kate leave the room.

She tried to get comfortable then she remembered the message she planned to write. As she picked up the paper and pencil from the nightstand, the hairs at the nape of her neck prickled. A chill ran up her spine. There was writing on the paper, mirror-image writing. Slowly she swung her legs over the side of the bed and sat there for a minute until the room stopped spinning. Then she walked to the mirror, almost afraid to look. She waited for a moment then held the message up to the mirror.

Find my grave...set me free...
Northwest corner of cemetery...please...!
M M

I knew it wasn't over, Mary Lou thought as she sat back down on the bed. But she couldn't go out there now. Whenever she tried to get up her knees buckled under her. I'll do it as soon as I'm better, she thought falling back on the bed. Now I'm too tired; I need rest. She lay down and fell asleep almost immediately.

An hour later Miss Dillard knocked at the door. "Miss Hammond, I've come to check on you." There was no answer. She knocked again, calling louder. "Mary Louise, are you all right? It's Miss Dillard." Again, no answer. She heard music coming from inside the room. She knocked again then turned the knob and found the door unlocked. The bed was empty; the sheet and blanket trailed across the floor. A music box on the dresser played a tune. She ignored that and looked around. The open dresser drawer seemed to say that someone dressed in a hurry. The closet door also stood open. The winter coats were gone. Where was Mary Lou?

"Where did she go? She was told to stay in bed. If she went outside, she could be in real trouble. It looks like she took off in rather a hurry." Miss Dillard nervously talked to no one in particular as she surveyed the room. It wasn't like Mary Lou to do something foolish when she was ill. After checking the bathroom, she decided to find Kate and question her. As the instructor, she was responsible for these girls' welfare. If Mary Lou had done something foolish, they must find her right away. She remembered the snowstorm and shuddered to think of what might have happened.

Outside the wind resumed its onslaught; the snow began to fall again in huge flakes. The wet snow slapped Mary Lou's face as she staggered toward the cemetery. She tied the woolen scarf around her nose and throat to protect her from the cold, but she still coughed with every breath she took. She was in a daze, neither awake nor sleeping. She wasn't sure what she was doing. All she knew was that she had to find the grave at the northwest corner of the cemetery.

Got to find the grave; got to set her free; then I'll be free, too. She clutched the prayer book in her hand; the other held the scarf tightly around her mouth. She felt feverish again. A band seemed to be tightening around her head. The sandpaper scraped her throat. Every cough sent a pain through her chest.

Got to find the grave... got to find the grave....

She rattled the locked cemetery gate trying desperately to get inside, but the lock wouldn't budge. When she looked around all Mary Lou could see were mounds of snow. Which way is north? I think it's this way. She held onto the fence as she pulled herself along it. When she reached a corner she looked up at the sky trying to see where the sun was, but all she saw were clouds and more snow falling. She tried to clear her head. Okay, if this is north, west should be on the left. She kept plodding along the fence through the drifting blowing snow, oblivious to the danger. She knew only one thing: she had to find the grave.

The corner, here it is. She stopped and took labored breaths holding on to the fence to keep from falling. But how would she get inside? She couldn't climb over; she was too weak. She squinted her eyes and saw the top of a tombstone sticking out from the snow. If she put her hand through the slats, she might just be able to reach it. There, she touched the stone and began rubbing her mitten against the granite. I can't read it. It's all icy. She rubbed harder. Her body felt numb from the cold. I'm so tired, she thought. All I want to do is sleep. A blast of cold wind renewed her efforts. She rubbed as hard as she could until finally she made out a few letters.

MA———ET MON———UE
1866-1911

"I found it," she croaked. "The grave! It's really true. She did exist."

Mary Lou opened the prayer book. In barely a whisper she began to read.

"Child of God, release this earthly prison.
Fly to Heaven on the wings of a dove.
You are the blessed of the Father.
His kingdom awaits you."

Then, through tears of sorrow she said, "Go Margaret, you're free. Go home."

Nothing happened. Mary Lou felt herself slipping down to the ground, numb with cold and exhaustion. I'm going to die out here, she thought. Oh God, I don't want to freeze to death.

"Margaret Montague," she called weakly. "Can you hear me?" Are you here?" Her throat was so sore, she could barely croak. She became angry. "You stubborn woman! I've done all this for you, risked my life and my sanity. Let go and get out of here, now." Her voice failed and her strength with it. She leaned back against the fence. Suddenly the snow swirled around assuming the vague form of a woman. Mary Lou squeezed her eyes shut then opened them again. The form lingered just above the grave.

"Margaret," Mary Lou croaked. "Is that you? Go. Please go. Be free and set me free, too."

The form encircled Mary Lou for a moment covering her with a warm friendly feeling. Then it drifted away. Margaret Montague was free.

Mary Lou breathed a sigh of relief. It's over, she thought. This nightmare is over. I'm so tired. I'll just rest here for a few minutes before I go back.

A gray shape came slinking toward her. For a moment she was frightened. The ghost cat—does it mean I'm going to die? Then the animal curled its body around her chest and throat. Mary Lou breathed in the warm air through the cat's fur. "You're not a ghost at all," she whispered. "You're trying to protect me. It's warm here in the snow, warm and soft." She closed her eyes and fell into a mesmerized sleep. In a few moments the snow began covering her inert form.

Chapter 36

"Miss Stevens, where is Mary Lou Hammond?" Miss Dillard asked pulling Kate away from her duties.

"I left her in our room. She's going to stay in bed all day. Why?" Kate's eyes widened with fear.

"She's not there now."

"Where is she?" Kate asked.

"That's what I want to know. Her coat is missing and the room is a mess. What happened?"

"I don't know." Kate grabbed her coat and ran to the nurses' home, Miss Dillard close behind. The wind hit them with a frigid fist as they left the building.

I hope she didn't go anywhere in this weather, Kate thought. But where would she have gone? She knew she was supposed to rest. Oh God! She's not responsible for her actions. In the state she's in, anything could happen.

Kate gasped as she entered the room. A chill ran up her arms as she heard the music box playing. She quickly closed the lid. This was not like Lulu. Something was wrong. She looked around wildly, searching for some clue as to where she might be. Then she saw it, on the nightstand. She grabbed the note and ran to the mirror.

"Look, Miss Dillard.

"What is it?" the instructor asked looking at the mirror-image writing. Her eyes widened as she read the words.

"This is where she went," Kate said.

"But why?"

Kate shook her head. "She's obsessed with freeing the ghost."

"Oh dear God, in this storm. Quick, get some blankets; bundle up and meet me downstairs. I'll call Dr. Corbett. We're going to need him."

Ten minutes later the trio headed for the cemetery, heads down bucking the fierce wind and swirling snow. They held hands so as not to lose one another.

Kate kept tripping in the masses of snow. Jack Corbett pulled her up and gripped her tight. "I can't see a thing, no landmarks. Which way do we go?"

"We have to find the power plant," Miss Dillard shouted. The cemetery is behind it."

They trudged on, heads bent down bucking the wind. After what seemed like hours they came to the power plant.

"Stop a minute," Jack said. "Let's take a breath and get our bearings."

Martha Dillard looked around. She had come to this old cemetery so many times that she knew the way blindfolded. And that was practically what they were now. "This way," she commanded.

"Here's the gate," Kate shouted. "But it's locked."

"Let's head for the northwest corner," Miss Dillard called. "That's probably where she went."

"Which way is northwest?" Kate asked.

"I think it's this way," Jack answered pulling her behind him.

They stumbled clutching the wooden fence as they moved painstakingly slow.

"Look, I see something, or someone, huddled in the snow," Jack shouted picking up the pace. He saw a pair of yellow eyes look up at him as the cat slipped away.

Jack knelt down beside the half-frozen figure brushing the snow away from her face. "Give me a blanket."

"Is she alive?" Miss Dillard asked.

"Yes, she's breathing. Another hour out here and she wouldn't be."

Kate began to cry, oblivious to the tears freezing on her cheeks.

"This is no time for sniveling," Jack said. "Help me wrap her up."

Kate jumped to the task. Together the three wrapped Mary Lou in the woolen blankets. Dr. Corbett lifted her in his arms and began the trek back, Kate and Miss Dillard guiding him. The trip seemed endless. The snow was beginning to slacken. Their footprints were just visible. They followed them until they finally saw the buildings looming ahead.

"We'll take her right to the infirmary," he said.

The women followed his instructions, opening doors, while Miss Dillard shouted instructions to the staff.

It wasn't long before Mary Lou lay in a warm bed, her pinched face white as death. She coughed ominously. Jack listened to her chest, frowning. He peered into the swollen red throat. The thermometer registered ninety-six degrees.

"She's suffering from hypothermia," he said. "Get some hot water bottles around her body, but don't let them directly touch her skin," he ordered. He wrapped a towel snuggly around her head. "Our first priority it to get her body temperature back up to normal," he said talking to himself as well as the staff. "Another blanket here, please."

Mary Lou began to respond to the voices around her. "Where...? What...?" she murmured.

"Can you swallow something warm?" Jack asked.

"I—I think so."

He motioned to the nurse who quickly returned with warm sweetened tea. She held Mary Lou's head as she carefully sipped it through chattering teeth.

"We'll get penicillin into her now," Jack said as he wrote the order for injections every four hours.

The nurse on duty gave the first one into Mary Lou's small bottom. She winced as the needle penetrated deep into the muscle, but didn't complain.

"She's sure going to have a sore behind after a few of these," the nurse said.

"She'll be lucky if that's all she has," Jack said. "Why did she go out there? God, she really believes in that ghost story."

"I'm afraid so," Miss Dillard said shaking her head. "Mary Louise, can you hear me?"

"Miss Dillard?" she whispered. "Where am I? What happened?"

"We found you at the cemetery, half frozen. What were you doing out there?"

"I don't remember going there I don't remember anything."

"The note, Lulu," Kate said looking anxiously down at her friend. "We found the note."

"The note. Now I remember. I found the note and I found her grave. I saw her. I actually saw her. Now she's free. Won't haunt me any more." With those words she drifted into a restful sleep.

"What's her temperature now?" Jack asked, running his hand through his hair.

"Ninety-nine point eight," the nurse answered.

"Good. It'll probably continue to climb but, at least, we won't have to worry about hypothermia anymore." He looked down at the sleeping girl and shook his head.

Chapter 37

Within a few days Mary Lou began to feel human again. The nightmare was finally over and she would soon leave Hillside for good.

"Miss Hammond," the nurse poked her head around the curtain, "you have a phone call." She hesitated for a moment. "I'm not supposed to let patients use the phone at the nurses' station, but your case is different." She gave Mary Lou a collaborative wink. "Can you make it?"

"I think so," Mary Lou said as she winced sitting up. "My butt is really sore."

"I know," the nurse said. "Let me help you." She took her arm and guided her to the desk. "This chair is pretty comfortable," she said helping Mary Lou to sit down.

"Ouch." She shifted her weight so that she was not sitting on the area of the last injection.

"I'll give you some privacy." The nurse walked off to check on her other patients.

"Hello," Mary Lou said.

"Hi, it's Bill. How are you doing?"

He sounded distant, his voice strained. "I'm a lot better. Dr. Corbett will be around later and he may release me today."

"What exactly does that mean?" he asked.

"Well, I can go back to my room and leave this weekend with all my class-mates."

"Oh." He hesitated for so long that she thought they had been disconnected. "Um, you see, I can't pick you up this weekend. I'm busy."

Mary Lou bristled. Busy? I'm supposed to be your girlfriend. She pursed her lips and said in a clipped tone, "Don't worry about it. Kate's parents will take me back. I've decided not to go home to

Rockford. We're supposed to report for class at St. Benedict's on Monday morning and I don't feel up to that long bus ride. I'll call my mother and explain."

"Okay," he said with obvious relief in his voice.

"There's something else, isn't there?" she asked. Since he didn't answer right away, she decided to take the initiative. "I've been lying here thinking about the future. I don't think we should see each other for a while. This experience has—changed me. I need to sort things out and you do, too. So why don't we put our relationship on hold for now."

"I'm glad you said that, because I've been thinking the same thing."

She heard the relief in his voice. You coward, she thought bitterly. You didn't have the guts to come right out and tell me.

"I have to get off this phone now, Bill. Why don't you call me in a few weeks, okay?"

"Sounds good. I'm glad you're better and got that ghost business out of your system."

"Yeah." If you only knew. "Goodbye Bill." She placed the receiver back in its cradle and heaved a mixed sigh of relief and sorrow. Then she pushed herself off the chair and shuffled back to her bed.

An hour later Jack Corbett came in, his smile fading as he looked at her face. "Red eyes? Tears? What's wrong?"

She swallowed hard and took a deep breath. "I just broke up with my boy-friend."

"I'm sorry."

"I'm not. I never realized how self-centered he is until all this started. All he could think of was how it affected his life."

"Then you're better off without him." He rubbed his hand over his chin and looked down at her. "I'd say you've done a lot of growing up in these three months." He smiled and took her wrist, feeling the strong steady pulse.

She nodded, unable to say anything more.

"According to your chart, your temperature has been normal for the past forty-eight hours," he said. "Open wide and let me see that throat." Gently he examined her throat, probed her lymph glands, and listened to her lungs.

"All clear," he said removing the stethoscope. "We can stop the injections and I'll write your discharge. How's the cough?"

"Much better. In fact it's almost gone."

"Good. Now, Mary Hammond, I'll say goodbye for now and wish you a happy successful life. And, I hope you have no more encounters with the supernatural." He smiled, shook her hand and held it for a moment.

"Thanks for believing in me. No more ghosts. And, good luck in your research." She watched him walk to the desk almost wishing for a future with him. No, I'm not ready for anything like that, she told herself, not for a long time.

"Wasn't that Dr. Corbett I saw at the nurses' station?" Kate asked bouncing into the room.

"He's discharged me. Isn't that great?"

"Yeah, but why are your eyes all swollen and there's a catch in your voice."

Tears sneaked out of the corners of Mary Lou's eyes. She took a tissue out of the box at the bedside and blew her nose. "I broke up with Bill."

"You what?" Kate's eyes widened and her mouth dropped open.

"You heard me."

Kate sat down on the edge of the bed just looking at her friend. "You know, I've been talking to him while you were so sick and he did sound kind of—I don't know, like there was something holding him back."

"Well, we both decided to put things on hold for a while. It's for the best. Bill is wrapped up in Bill." She looked away and swallowed hard again, but was determined not to waste any more tears on him.

Kate took her friend's hand. "Lulu, I'm sorry."

"I'm not," Mary Lou said. "I feel relieved. I realize that he would have controlled me, just like my mother has all these years." She shook her head. "You know Miss Dillard said a strange thing when she talked to me a few weeks ago. She said, 'life is a banquet. Savor it.' I can't get those words out of my head. It was as if she regretted not doing just that."

"That sounds good to me," Kate said. "Start with the crackers and cheese and go all the way to the dessert."

Mary Lou laughed. "Leave it to you to think of food. Anyway, I've made a decision. After we graduate and take State Boards, I'm not going home to Rockford."

"You're not? I can't believe you." Kate stared with her mouth open again.

"I'm going to stay in Chicago and work in one of the teaching hospitals. Maybe I'll share an apartment with someone." She looked at Kate expectantly.

"Let's do it together," Kate squealed. "We'll strike out on our own."

"I was hoping you'd say that. There's one other favor I have to ask you. When your parents pick you up Friday night, do you think they'd drop me off at St. Benedict's?"

"Oh no," Kate said adamantly. "You're coming home with me. We'll spend the weekend at my house. My mom will pamper you. She's good at that."

Mary Lou's eyes welled up again. "You're the best," she whispered. She hesitated then said, "Another decision I've made is to call myself Mary Hammond and use only the middle initial. Mary Lou sounds too childish." She visualized a name pin clipped to a brand new uniform: Mary L. Hammond, RN.

"Boy, you're full of surprises today." Kate shook her head and stared at her friend. Then her expression turned sheepish. "Can I still call you Lulu?"

Mary Lou threw back her head and laughed. It felt so good. "Of course. To you I'll always be Lulu." She took her friend's hand and gave it a squeeze.

"How was the final exam?" Mary Lou asked. "I've been worried about it.

"Not too bad," Kate said. "I'm sure Dill Pickle will let you make it up."

At that moment a disheveled head peaked around the corner followed by a scrawny body swathed in a huge black cape. Mary Lou giggled when she saw Josephine. The woman stood for a moment, a solemn expression on her face. In her hand she carried an artificial daisy, the stem bent to the side. The flower, too, looked sad. One foot in front of the other, Josephine walked slowly up to the bed, and then placed the flower gently on Mary Lou's chest. She clasped her hands and stepped back. Then she grinned and raised her eyebrows. "Are you gonna die?" she whispered, a look of expectation on her face.

"No, the doctor said I'm doing fine and can go home soon. Thank you for the flower."

Josephine scrunched up her face in disappointment. "You sent the ghost away, but there's another one. I saw it, just this morning." She twirled around and made a soft 'whooing' sound. "It has sharp claws and red eyes."

"I'm sure there are a lot of ghosts around here, but I'm through with them," Mary Lou said. "Good-bye Josephine, I'll miss you and I'll never forget you."

Without another word, the woman circled around three times and ran out of the room humming an unidentifiable tune.

"She's a real character," Kate said, laughing.

"She's harmless and sort of endearing. Oh, here comes Miss Dillard," Mary Lou said reaching out her free hand in greeting.

"How are you this evening, Mary Louise? Your eyes look bright and your color's good. I do believe you're almost well."

"Dr. Corbett said I'm practically fit as a fiddle. But my bottom is going to be sore for weeks." Mary Lou grimaced.

"That's a small price to pay. We could have lost you, you know." Miss Dillard looked at her with an almost affectionate gaze.

Mary Lou frowned. "When can I make up the final exam?" she asked clutching the bedclothes.

"Since your grades have improved and you've done all the assigned papers, I've decided to exempt you from the final exam, in view of the circumstances. The rest of your class took it today."

Mary Lou breathed a sigh of relief. "How can I thank you? I've been lying here worrying and wondering about it."

"I think that's the least we can do after the experience you've had here. You can't imagine the rumors that are going around, about you being mesmerized by the ghost that stalks this place. I'm sure it will grow into a legend, exaggerated every time it's retold." She looked at the two young people and smiled.

"That ghost won't roam around here anymore. She's free," Mary Lou said. "And I'll never forget these three months as long as I live." She looked from Miss Dillard to Kate. "And I'm free, too."

"I'll leave you now. I just wanted to tell you that Dr. Corbett has written your release. You can go back to your room at any time."

Mary Lou grinned, feeling truly liberated for the first time since she had come to this place.

"Good bye, Mary Louise Hammond," Miss Dillard said. "I'll certainly remember you." Their eyes met and held for a moment. "Be happy, my dear."

"I'll never forget you, Miss Dillard. Thank you for believing in me."

Martha Dillard walked slowly out of the infirmary without looking back. Then she straightened and hurried along. There was much work to do. Sunday night a new group of students would be arriving. She must be sure everything was ready. The circle would continue at Hillside and she would be entrenched in it for the rest of her life.

Epilogue

The old buildings are gone, relegated to the wrecker's ball, their dust mingling with the earth. But their essence remains. The vibrations of years of existence in this limbo are still there, for those who can feel them.

There are no more wet sheet packs, sedation tubs, nor salt glow. Although Electroconvulsive Therapy is still used in certain cases, it is administered under anesthesia. Insulin Coma Therapy and prefrontal lobotomy are only referred to in the archives of psychiatric history.

Modern drugs are now available to sedate agitated patients, elevate mood in those who are depressed, and enable the mentally ill to live on their own. But many of these people do not easily fit into society. We see them surviving on the streets of major cities and in many prisons. These are the forgotten ones, those who once lived in state hospitals. Today no one remembers people like Josephine and Rosie except those nurses who spent their psychiatric rotations there. But, in the still of the night one may hear a howl, a cackling laugh or a tinkling piano, for these memories are part of the atmosphere and the earth.

The End

About the Author

Helen Osterman lives in a suburb of Chicago. She has five children and nine grandchildren. Helen received a Bachelor of Nursing degree from Mercy Hospital-St. Xavier College. During her training, she spent three months at Chicago State Mental Hospital for her psychiatric rotation. Years later, she earned a Master's Degree from Northern Illinois University.

Throughout her forty-five year nursing career, Helen wrote articles for both nursing and medical journals, including *Geriatric Nursing*, *Nursing Management*, *Orthopaedic Nursing* and *Nursing Spectrum*. She wrote a section for *Clinics in Podiatric Medicine and Surgery* in 1997.

In 1997 and 1998, she published two short novels about a nurse, *The Web* and *Things Hidden*, by Vista Publishing: a nurse owned publishing company.

Helen is also the author of the Emma Winberry Mystery series: *The Accidental Sleuth*, 2007 and *The Stranger in the Opera House*, 2009.

Helen is a member of The American Association of University Women, The Mystery Writers of America and Sisters in Crime.

Her web site is: www.helenosterman.com.

LaVergne, TN USA
21 September 2010
197870LV00003B/18/P